T0128874

The Street Gangs of Euroburg

A Story of Research

Malcolm W. Klein

iUniverse, Inc.
New York   Bloomington

The Street Gangs of Euroburg
A Story of Research

iUniverse books may be ordered through booksellers or by contacting:

iUniverse
1663 Liberty Drive
Bloomington, IN 47403
www.iuniverse.com
1-800-Authors (1-800-288-4677)

Because of the dynamic nature of the Internet, any Web addresses or
links contained in this book may have changed since publication and
may no longer be valid. The views expressed in this work are solely those
of the author and do not necessarily refl ect the views of the publisher,
and the publisher hereby disclaims any responsibility for them.

ISBN: 978-1-4401-0983-6 (pbk)
ISBN: 978-1-4401-0984-3 (ebk)

Printed in the United States of America

iUniverse Rev. Date: 1/19/2009

"In social research, person and method are not random. One's preferences reflect one's view of 'science', of 'reality', and how to judge them – and to some extent, one's ethics."

Martin W. Keller

Table of Contents

Preface: Fact and Fiction

While on a gang research trip to Australia, I related my interest in branching out from academic to fictional writing to Morris West, the famous novelist and mystery writer, author of *The Shoes of the Fisherman, Proteus, The Ambassador, The Tower of Babel* and a myriad other stories. West and I and our wives were invited dinner guests, and he took it upon himself to mentor me, however briefly, on some of his tricks of the fiction trade.

"First," he said, "make sure you write in the language of your readers; write to engage their age group, their interests, their experiences so you can bring them along with you."

"Second, learn to steal from others." I reacted immediately with shock at the implication for plagiarism, but he followed quickly with "Take in the words and incidents of other people. They've experienced more than you, so listen to them and incorporate their experiences into your story."

Mr. West was in his early eighties at the time, and therefore a man of wisdom. I am approaching that same period myself, so I listened then and remember now. My story, in the coming pages, incorporates the experiences of others.

However, if you read this book as a novel, I will have failed. I'm not that kind of writer.

If you read this book as an academic exercise in doing comparative street gang research, I will have succeeded only partially. My colleagues and I have written that exercise elsewhere, and extensively.

In these pages I offer a combination of fact and fiction designed to help you appreciate the advantages of comparative gang research. But I also want to show that such research takes place in the contexts of human strengths and frailties and the settings in which these are played out. Writing in this fashion has been a severe challenge – where is Morris West when you need him – but I've enjoyed it immensely.

My city, Euroburg, is fictional, but it is an amalgam of many European cities that have experienced street gang problems. Some readers will find elements from Stockholm and Oslo, Frankfurt and Berlin and Stuttgart, Amsterdam and The Hague, London and Manchester, Madrid and Barcelona, along with Zurich, Moscow, Brussels, and Athens. They have been incorporated into Euroburg.

Professor Keller's research team is fictional, but it too is an amalgam, in this case of gang researchers I have known and worked with. No team member is based on only one individual. If my colleagues find bits of themselves in the team, I hope they will be tolerant; there are bits of me in there as well.

The findings of Keller's project are also fictional, but they are based on research data from many studies undertaken by colleagues in the Eurogang Program. Despite variations in city and nation, there are far more similarities among street gangs in these places than there are differences. Findings from one location often mirror findings from others. Thus there can be a *science* of street gangs. In that spirit, I have included several Special Comments from the Author, labeled Background Statements, which provide summaries of relevant research. These are in Chapter 5, 12, 14, 17, and 28.

Finally, the descriptions of most places and incidents offered in this book are *not* fictional. Only their simultaneous placement in Euroburg is fictional. They have been lifted from their origins and given new life in this composite city. They could be found in any city, any nation, at any time since around 1980.

So yes, I have "stolen", especially from my valued colleagues in the Eurogang Program. This was not my original intention, just as this book was not. But over the ten years since the Program's inception at a meeting in Leuven, Belgium, I have retained notes taken from a dozen workshops and meetings, emails and faxes, and memories of many, many conversations, some with beer and wine and a few not.

Of course, many of my American research colleagues and students and staff members over forty years are here in bits and pieces borrowed, but never reproduced in whole. My "thefts", I would tell Morris West, are jigsaw pieces cut and mixed in new patterns that are real but hopefully not too recognizable.

For ten years, I have been privileged to work with scores of European and American colleagues under the umbrella of a fascinating and challenging enterprise. It is known as the Eurogang Program. Almost 200 scholars and officials have been involved, mostly on a volunteer basis. I am grateful to them for their persistence. In particular, I acknowledge the working group leaders and members of the Steering Committee: Americans Cheryl Maxson, Jody Miller, Finn Esbensen and Scott Decker along with Europeans Inger-Lise Lien, Frank van Gemert, Frank Weerman, Juanjo Medina, Judith Aldridge, Toré Bjorgo, and Elmar Weitekamp. They stand in for all the others, and they are, indeed, my very good friends. Thank you, colleagues and friends. And special thanks to Cheryl Maxson, Margy Gatz, and Frank Weerman for their very extensive review and critique of this manuscript's first draft. They were both helpful and unaccountably enthusiastic. Finally, I am pleased to acknowledge the financial support of the Office of the Provost at the University of Southern California in bringing this manuscript to its publication.

Malcolm W. Klein
Los Angeles, 2008

Light →
Industry 16

Light
Industry

The "Middle East"

Fort Araby

The Village

16

16

Rapids

Power
Station

16

Seng Chin?
Joechile

Ah ban
Cafe

16

12

16 to 18th
Century
Houses

1

13

Mixed New and Old
Residential District

2

Old Guild Halls
District

Piers
Euro

14 Wharse

5

Canal
Docks

14

Backwater
Canals
Dist.

4

6

7

Old
Town

16

9

RR

11

14

EUROBURG

1. Grand Park
2. Castle
3. Castle Gardens
4. Toll House / c
5. Police Headquarters
6. Town Hall
7. Central Square
8. St. Agnes
9. R.R. Station
10. Roman Museum
11. Fine Arts Museum
12. Monastery Hill

13. Bomber with
14. Roman Ruins
15. Rapids Power Station
16. Subway Stations

N
W   E
S

RR

RR

1. The Trigger

From the Euroburg Daily News, June 18, by Patrick van der Waal:

Police reports of young predators mugging tourists and committing smash-and-grab burglaries over the past several days were the subject of a special news briefing yesterday at the central police headquarters. Following an introduction by Police Chief Schmidt, Sergeant André Mellers, head of a special gang unit established several years ago, outlined the problem.

"There is an ugly pattern to these vicious crimes," reported Sgt. Mellers. According to Mellers, "gang warfare" and "organized gang crime" have broken out as a result of rival gangs' attempts to control criminal territories in the central city, even though "the gangsters do not even reside there." Additional officers will be assigned, Mellers indicated, to gather sensitive intelligence on gang members and gang organizations. Meanwhile, he said, a "zero tolerance" approach will be taken toward the presence of gang members in downtown Euroburg, especially in the tourist-heavy Old Town area.

After the news conference, this reporter questioned several people about the problem. "What we've got to do," said one police official, "is what you do about cockroaches and other vermin; you get someone in there to do whatever they can to get rid of the creatures."

"What the f---- does that mean," retorted Mohammed H., a purported leader of a youth group known as The Smokes. "Seems like the cops are gonna wage war on groups they invented just to justify their own control over the city."

From the Euroburg Daily News, June 19, by Patrick van der Waal:

Following the announcement of a police crackdown on street gangs, various individuals and groups responded to the allegation that the city is facing a major gang problem. Said Professor Martin Keller, a criminologist at the Free University of Euroburg, "We've had some troublesome youth groups for some years now and there is no reason to believe the problem is going to go away. Chief Schmidt has been here almost four years, during which he has shown little interest or understanding of such groups." An official from the Mayor's office, who oversees police operations in Euroburg, noted "When the cop goes down the street in his car or on foot, he may own that street for the moment. But when he's off the street, the gangs fill in right behind him unless there's another cop right around the corner. We don't have enough officers to prevent this."

Said Alexander A., a street worker assigned to a group or gang called The Zealots, "I don't think the mayor or the police understand these groups at all. They're demonizing them. Well, I've gotten close to the demons, and they're just marginalized immigrant kids trying to find some identity for themselves."

When this reporter checked with the Mayor's office about these conflicting views, a spokeswoman indicated the Mayor's intention to call a meeting of city officials and others to discuss an anti-gang strategy for the city, including as well professional criminologists from the university. "Ah," Professor Martin Keller told this reporter; "Grist for the researcher's mill."

From the Euroburg Daily News, June 25, by Patrick van der Waal:

In response to reports of increased street gang violence in downtown Euroburg, the Mayor's office has announced an emergency meeting for June 27 at City Hall to evaluate the problem and appropriate responses. In announcing the meeting, the Mayor's spokeswoman noted that gang problems previously centered around housing developments in the outskirts of the city now seem to be encroaching on the central city and Old Town areas. "We cannot allow this," she said. "These troublesome youths don't live in these areas which are critical to our economic stability, and they certainly don't look as though they belong here."

2. The Political Response

June 27 was the weekly market day in the town square. By ten o'clock in the morning scores of stalls, tents, and open displays filled much of the square. Tourists taking pictures had to stand on one of the two statues, either the pedestal of the obelisk stolen from ancient Egypt by the conquering Romans, or the River Fountain, as it was called: eight water sprites and assorted fishes all spouting small streams of water under the gaze of a Neptune replica dressed mostly in fish net. The water, it is said, comes directly from the Euro-Canal, so warning signs not to drink the water are posted in half a dozen languages – English, European, and Eastern.

Market Day in Euroburg.

The Mayor's panel members would be delayed by stalls of odoriferous fish, hanging meat and game, fruits and vegetables, and every imaginable assortment of inexpensive clothing, toys, souvenirs, questionable antiques, CDs, and so on. Throngs of photo-op tourists, shopping housewives, lunch hounds and pick-pocketing youth wind through the mazes, each intent on a different pursuit. The town hall looms above all this on the north side of the square, built of local limestone and half-timbering. Often reconstructed after river floods, invasions, and the bombings of World War II, it retains its 15th century ambience and, miraculously, its 16th century tower clock and calendar. The clock comes alive at noon and 6:00 p.m. as little doors open and costumed knights and ladies come out, bow, and return in a Sid Caesar-like skit. The clock chimes hourly – most of the time – although 6:00 p.m. seems to have lost one of its bells.

Across the square is the Cathedral of Saint Agnes, always partly covered by scaffolding that looks as old as the church itself. The Bishop's House, actually constructed before the Cathedral (some things can't wait) is another half-timbered edifice but now a four-star business and tourist hotel. On the other two sides of the square are arcades built out far enough to shelter half a dozen outdoor cafes, while inside are various boutiques, souvenir shops, up-scale stores and, in the far corner, a McDonalds built to resemble a small chateau with golden arches. Political graffiti and tags can be seen on its side walls.

The police are here, too, wandering nonchalantly through the market maze and arcades, their eyes constantly surveying local youths and occasional gypsy vendors. As is so often the case in Europe, the police are non-intrusive, establishing a presence but not order. Indeed, the whole setting is festive and evocative of earlier times when the bishop and the guilds set the tone of the town. The idea that town hall today would feature a panel on street gangs seemed incongruous, at the least.

The interior of town hall captures its exterior. High, beamed ceilings connect wood-paneled walls with historical paintings of battles and countryside, a mock 16th century map of the early town when the canal was being built, regional flags and portraits of forgotten local celebrities. A wide wooden staircase leads up to interior oaken doors that hide the modern offices inside. To the left is the council chamber, in which the mayor's panel assembled at a wide dais before seating for a hundred or more townspeople. Today, only thirty to forty were in attendance, many sporting the shopping bags filled from the prior hours in the market.

Behind the dais is another set of regional flags and a painting of a Roman fort built on the hill overlooking the old flood plain that now includes the canal. Over a dozen very modern looking men – all men, it should be noted

– sat in a row, each in coat and tie, each behind a small microphone, with a plastic cup and plastic liter of bottled water. In the middle sat the mayor who opened the meeting with a pro forma recitation of city pride and the dangers posed by unlawful youthful behavior. Then he turned matters over to the deputy mayor so that he could attend "yet another important civic function" (unbeknownst to the audience, the latter was taking place in the basement Rathskeller).

Panel members included Police Chief Schmidt and his gang unit sergeant, André Mellers, two members of the city council and the city accountant, the head of Council of Euroburg Businessmen, the deputy director of the city school system and his chief security officer, the director of the city youth commission, a priest, a lawyer attached to the young adults court, a director of a not-for-profit youth agency, a regional representative of the National Ministry of Immigration, and Professor Martin Keller. Off to the side were a few assistants and Daily News reporter Patrick van der Waal.

The ensuing statements and discussion were more or less predictable, and through most of the allotted two hours not very illuminating. Chief Schmidt noted the need to maintain order in the central city, and assured the audience that the youth crime was not a gang problem.

"We don't have gangs in Euroburg. I've been to seminars run by the International Association of Police Chiefs, where gang experts from cities like Los Angeles and Chicago have described their criminal street gangs. We don't have that here. At worst, we have a few delinquent youth groups that just bother each other and come to Old Town to create trouble. But with more resources, we can deter them; we just need for the mayor and city council to provide the money for more officers, and maybe give us some laws that target group crime as a conspiracy."

Sergeant Mellers, following the chief, agreed that gang problems certainly were not like those in America, but noted that his unit was maintaining surveillance on several youth groups, mostly from the outskirts, that had "gang-like propensities" as he put it. "But I agree with the chief," he said. "We can handle them if we get the support we need."

Other panelists chimed in to support the call for more police resources. The school officials and businessmen's spokesman were particularly supportive. Others and the agency representatives were concerned that "criminalizing youthful behavior," as the priest stated the issue, overlooked the root causes of youth crime. Racism, immigration issues, absence of meaningful youth job opportunities, and cultural patterns were all raised as matters to be considered in a "balanced approach".

The chief responded with the suggestion that if parents were more attentive to their own children, none of these concerns would need all this discussion. "But some of our local boys, and many of those in the housing developments, are allowed to run loose because their parents are either not around or too occupied with their own problems."

At the point that the panel began to deteriorate into competing ideologies, the city accountant stepped in to assure everyone that if a strategy to combat the problem could be developed, the city treasury could certainly support meaningful action steps. The deputy mayor then intervened, reading from a script that seemed to have been prepared ahead of time.

The mayor, he reported, had already consulted with various people about steps that could be taken to understand the seriousness of the youth crime problem. Suggestions had been offered, such as a police task force to crack down on youth groups; a "gang czar" to organize the city's response; an ad hoc committee of the city council to take testimony and devise a plan; appointment of a "commission of experts" to discuss the problem; and a research study by "our own university experts." The mayor, he repeated, was inclined toward the university option because any task force or council committee or commission would have to engage the university's crime experts in any case.

And then, just to prove that the mayor was fully in charge (and the panel discussion, perhaps, was mere window-dressing), the deputy mayor indicated that the National Ministry of Justice, the National Ministry of Immigration, and the city accountant had already been engaged by the mayor's office in discussions to fund a university-based study of gangs and crime in Euroburg.

The awkward silence that followed this announcement was broken by Prof. Keller who, up to that time, had done little more than puff at his pipe and take notes on a long pad of yellow legal paper. But now the affair turned into the Martin Keller show.

"Let me say, first, that this comes as a surprise to me – a complete surprise. I was even surprised to be invited here today; city officials are seldom known to turn to university researchers to understand city problems. I guess I'm flattered, also, since somebody in the mayor's office must have read about our research at the Free University. I'm not sure how to respond, other than to say that if funds are made available to study youth or group crime in Euroburg, then I'm sure we can put such funds to good use.

"However, I should warn you all, panelists and audience alike, that I have some concerns about the kinds of conventional wisdoms people have about such matters. Research is often unkind to the conventional ways different people see crime issues. Let me just give you two examples.

"The first is the very article in our own Daily News ten days ago by Mr. van der Waal, the reporter sitting close to our panel today. That article quoted officials about a breakout of "gang warfare" and "organized gang crime". In the absence of supportive data that we can all review, I am frankly skeptical about such panicky reports.

"An American colleague of mine recently sent me a news report about a city that reported what police officials called 'skyrocketing gang crime,' an increase in one year from 145 to 413 gang incidents. But further investigation by the news reporter revealed that graffiti and vandalism alone accounted for a jump from 72 to 318 incidents, or fully 90 percent of the increase. In other words the 'skyrocketing gang crime' was a fizzle of scrawls on public walls and property. Here in Euroburg, I would urge that we hold off judgment about dramatic reports of gang crime until we can look together, and dispassionately, at just what is really going on.

"My second example, in direct contrast, comes from Chief Schmidt's assertion that we don't have street gangs in Euroburg, because our few 'delinquent youth groups' don't look like the notorious gangs of Los Angeles and Chicago. But recent reports from a large research enterprise called the Eurogang Program has suggested that most American gangs also don't look like the stereotypical image of Los Angeles and Chicago gangs; most American gangs are smaller, less organized, and less violent than those traditional big city street gangs in the United States. Well, if most American gangs are not so organized but nonetheless are properly defined as street gangs, then maybe we do have such gangs here in Euroburg. I submit to you that this is an open question, what my colleagues would call 'an empirical question', to be decided not by municipal defensiveness but by some careful research.

"In short, if the mayor's office and others are going to support a university study of the so-called gang problem here in our city, we should take on the challenge with truly open minds. We should wait to see what research data tell us before we jump at measures to respond to 'gang problems'. I can report to you already that most American programs to ameliorate gang problems – scores of preventive and enforcement programs – have produced little evidence of either success or failure. If we do find a problem here in Euroburg, we may have to devise our own local solutions to our own local problem, respecting our own youth in and around the city."

Prof. Keller's dissertation had a pronounced quieting effect on the day's discussion – almost. As panelists gathered their papers together and audience members began to leave their seats and turn to the exits, a one-man outburst broke the silence and the mood:

"I don't understand how you can leave here like this," came the voice of a young man in the rear of the council chambers. "Everyone up there on the panel is an adult, even some quite old adults, with official positions and big salaries. None of you is a youth, none of you is a kid with troubles, none of you has ever been accused of being a so-called gang member. Where is their voice? How can you make decisions about gang problems or even gang research, without hearing from the kids you're talking about? It's a sham!"

While most panel and audience members quickened their steps toward the exits, several held back. The deputy mayor demanded to know the young man's name. Sergeant Mellers asked what his gang affiliation was. And Keller, in response, introduced them to Heinrich, his loud and impolite graduate student and youth advocate. Heinrich got no answers to his questions – unless being ignored is one kind of answer – but he would certainly come to be known to them in the future. In time, Heinrich would again become all too salient in the public's mind, and reporter van der Waal would have another story to write.

3. Euroburg: Romans to Street Gangs

Immediately following the "Panel of Old Farts" as he described the town hall session to Liz on his cell phone, Heinrich headed for the Café Akbar to meet her and fill her in. Heinrich and Liz were fellow graduate students in the criminology department at the Free University of Euroburg's Faculty of Law. More than that, they were soul mates; he the brash advocate of all things anti-establishment, she the watchful monitor of everyday events and assigned by the Gods to control Heinrich. They had met at the Akbar many times, intrigued by the young men who were tolerated there by the elders. Liz was the only female allowed in (although usually at the sidewalk tables where man talk was less intense), and only because the elders appreciated her control over Heinrich.

This afternoon, although acknowledging the presence of their young Easterners, Heinrich and Liz were seated in a far corner. They needed to get their act together because unlike the "old farts" of the panel, they had come to know these local youth who gathered at the bar at the outlet of the connecting subway lines. These, they thought, were precisely the youth being "demonized" by the public officials and the police with their talk of warring gangs and criminals. And both students agreed; their salvation lay in the proposed research study to be assigned to Professor Keller – their professor. They would take their concern to his summer seminar, scheduled for the next week.

And so they did, but by the time of the first seminar gathering on July 3rd, Keller had already made the basic decision for them. He told the half-dozen graduate students enrolled in the summer session, fortuitously labeled Communities and Crime, that the topic would be street gang research, in line with the funding being promised through the Mayor's office. Any student wishing to pass on the gang project and pursue a different topic was welcome to do so by meeting with him individually, but the group session would concentrate on the gang issue. Led gratefully by Heinrich and Liz, four students joined the gang team to be formed. Two others chose to seek projects allowing for secondary analysis of existing data sets, an easier process promising quicker payoff and publication possibilities.

Keller then invited Heinrich and Liz to relate what they knew so far about the youth groups or gangs they had contacted in the housing projects on the northern outskirts, while at the same time he sketched out a map of the city on a huge white board covering much of the end of the room. Liz responded, saying their kids would be found in the projects toward the top right of the board. Known locally as "The Middle East" or "Arab Town", the area included two massive housing projects. The first, an ugly high rise complex, started to accommodate guest workers in the 1960s. The second, a sprawling two-story "village" thought to represent lessons learned from problems with the high rise, lay just to the east of the first. A second generation of guest workers and an increasing number of Muslim refugees were to be found in the Village. While the high rise was bereft of special facilities of any cultural value, and called Fort Araby by some, the Village sported a large middle-eastern market of both indoor and outdoor stalls, smoke shops, a hookah bar and pastry, tea and baklava mini-cafés, and two mosques. The high rise project was little more than a darkened holding area; the Village offered some sense of community. Neither was ever visited by other Euroburgers except the police and gourmands experimenting with Eastern foods. The latter were welcomed to the Village by the merchants; the police were barely tolerated in either setting. Police were an arm of the state, feared by the elders and avoided by the youth. So-called gangs lived in both areas, according to Liz, the "Smokes" in the high rise and the "Zealots" in the Village. This was mostly learned from Liz and Heinrich's visits to the Akbar Café, she noted: they had not spent much time as yet in the projects themselves. They felt, she said, "awfully white" in the Middle East. They weren't ready to report on the youth groups.

Most Euroburgers have limited contact with the Middle East because of its distances from both the downtown area and the newer (post-war) industrial area to the northwest. One subway line leads from the industrial area to the station (and the Akbar Café) just south of the Middle East, where a one-stop spur heads into the projects while the main line goes directly south, across the canal, and ends in the main train station. Euroburgers' exposure to ethnic diversity is largely limited to subway trips north from the station and then west to the industrial area. On board one finds a mixture of first and second generation immigrant Turks, Moroccans, West African blacks, and recent refugees from war torn areas of Bosnia and Kosovo along with increasing numbers from Afghanistan and Iraq. What could be a cosmopolitan city is pretty much merely a segregated one. The Arabs, say many indigenous locals, are in an unfortunate situation exaggerated by their own failure to adapt to the local society and language and disrespect for western values about work and social order. Residents from the projects see mostly racism, deliberate segregation, and disrespect for their cultural values and religion. Euroburg, it seems, is a mirror for scores of modern European cities in transition.

Of course, little of this is known to the tourists who support the city's economy and return home in praise of this "quaint old city." They shop in Old Town, take pictures in the town square, the cathedral, the castle, and the museums. They eat in specialty restaurants and take sight-seeing bus tours that seldom get to the north side of the city. Some follow their Fodor's Guide to the several locations of Roman ruins and learn, however sketchily, that Euroburg has a history.

From the third century on, as Rome began to feel threatened by tribes to the north, it established forts or army encampments on the south sides of rivers and valleys to hold off or merely discourage encroachments by the Barbarians. Such an encampment was built on the rise above a flood plain, and just above what is now the Euro Canal. Just west of Town Hall is the Roman Museum, built on the site of the old encampment and filled with artifacts taken from excavations there. The cathedral has a glassed-over foundation of Roman temple ruins later incorporated into the crypt. Other ruins, including a few mosaic floors of the baths, now at the base of Old Town, suggest the town growth that must have succeeded the original army encampment. Unfortunately, some of these ruins, exposed but not treasured, show a small war between modern political graffiti and the "tags" of local youth, for whom any blank wall is a challenge, no matter its age.

Thereafter, Euroburg was little more than a sleepy village and swamp until the 13th century when the church saw it as a site for development. A bishop was appointed. Bishops need cathedrals, and so the small church built over the Roman temple ruins became the site for the Cathedral of Saint Agnes. The original Romanesque design faded as it took almost 150 years for St. Agnes to be completed, Romanesque outside but eventually Gothic in the interior. To show their importance (and the political centrality of their church to the growing town), successive bishops arranged for frescoes now attributed to Giotto and Tepelo alongside 15th and 16th century paintings in the style of Boticelli, Rafael, and a series of lesser known German and Dutch muralists. Added in time were 17th century stained glass windows, some of them removed and preserved through the Second World War and then painstakingly reinstalled afterwards.

A good deal of Baroque detailing eventually yielded a gaudy interior to the once austere setting. The combination of styles is duly noted in the guidebooks, so the history of art and architecture in one stylistic confusion now draws more tourists and art students than it does worshippers. A plaque, pointed out to all, marks the spot when the very first construction was underway, where the newly appointed bishop fell through a collapsing floor during a banquet and was killed. His remains lie below the crypt, but no one knows quite where.

As planned by the church originally, St. Agnes became the symbol of political, ecclesiastical, and commercial power. Local leaders did not oppose the bishops. Euroburg became a city-state of its own in the early 14th century, but soon ran into competition with other burgeoning towns, some more powerful than Euroburg as they expanded their hegemony for mostly commercial and trade purposes. And so the local merchants pondered their fate and came upon a solution that changed the city's history forever. The local guilds pooled their resources and built a small canal from the river – just below the rapids that prohibited through traffic and periodically caused the flood plain to fill.

With the canal moving from the west to east fringes of town, merchants could now have continuous boat travel to and through Euroburg. A toll house built on a cliff on the north shore opposite the town center (now Old Town) brought a tariff from every river boat. Money came in, supplies came in directly, and Euroburg became a commercial center of some importance. The early canal was later greatly enlarged to accommodate larger river ships and barges, and it flows today as a central fixture of the city, with elaborate house boats on the northwest end and dinner boats just beyond the town square and Old Town. The old toll house has been altered, but above it lies the castle and gardens that signaled the exchange of political power from the bishops to the guild-supported Counts of Euroburg.

Aside from various city-state wars that seemed endemic to the area, two other events helped to shape modern Euroburg. One was World War II, which did not spare much of the city but led to its reconstitution as both an industrial center requiring cheap labor from immigrant populations and as a center for tourism to its historic and reproduced architectural center.

The other event was the Black Death, the bubonic plague that swept across Europe. In 1347, the plague was brought west along the trade routes by the Mongols, and then spread from port to port. Within three years, it ravaged from Venice to Sicily, from Marseille to Spain and England. Then it spread north to Scandinavia, and back east through Germany and Russia. In Euroburg, close to 50 percent of the population was wiped out.

The city recovered in time, as did most, but not some of its most successful groups. Confidence in the church, and of course the bishops like those of Euroburg, declined markedly as a result of the devastation, hastening the power of political figures, the guilds and the merchant class. Urban centers like Euroburg re-emerged with a different style. The upcoming years of the Renaissance can still be seen in St. Agnes Cathedral. And, as happened elsewhere, the spread of the plague was blamed on the Jews as the carriers. The Jews were both banned and burned. Their cemetery was destroyed, with tombstones removed as trophies. To this day, some of them can be seen in the outer walls of old houses, built in as decorations.

Despite this, at the start of the Second World War there were two synagogues in town. Police armed with automatic rifles now are positioned outside the larger, old synagogue recently defaced with swastikas and obscenities. The two synagogues once served several thousand people, but now only a few score on the holiest of days. A defiant quotation is scratched into the lintel of the smaller building: "How odd of God to choose the Jews." The history is not so different from that of many Euroburgs throughout Europe, but as one of Professor Keller's students warned Liz, the Muslims of Fort Araby could become the Jews of our time.

In the modern post-war era of Euroburg, two modes of transportation loom far more important than the cars and buses, the bikes and motor scooters, and even the train that connects the city to its nation and others. One of these is the two-line subway system. The other is the Euro Canal that both provides the conduit for all main river traffic and the dividing line between the old city and its new expansion.

A proper visitor will engage the canal with interest. At the northwest end, closest to the river, is a mélange of older and newer houseboats almost permanently tied to the quais on each side. Some are old and seedy, often double-parked; others are newer and well kept. Most at various times are embellished by lines of drying laundry, flower pots and small trees in their holders, barking dogs and flitting cats, bicycles locked to railings, and all manner of colors ranging from grungy grey and brown to bright trims of red, blue, yellow and green in the manner of Greek or Portuguese island ports.

Ships, barges, and weekly river tour boats bring their wealth through the passage between the houseboats, rocking them gently. They pass on toward town past the backwater canals, remnants of the earlier canal dredging and now a complex warren of small boat alleys twisting among low-rent housing and shops of only local value. The backwater canal area is avoided by Euroburgers and tourists alike, as evidence of what can happen to quaintness after centuries of neglect.

The canal then carries on, harboring cormorants, ducks, coots, swans, and the occasional heron. Barges off-load at the piers on the north shore where low derricks and trailer trucks await them, while pleasure craft and tourist boats swing over to the docks, in front of town square and Old Town. Plaques show the earlier flood levels up to 40 feet, well above the square and the lower floors of buildings. Commerce to the north and pleasure to the south. The train station beyond Old Town adds its passengers to the mix, making the south bank of the canal a busy haven for shoppers and sightseers. Passengers headed for Fort Araby or "The Village" and the industrial complex to the northwest can connect directly to the subway leaving from the train station.

The subway, then, is the other main artery of human traffic. Those heading for the industries stay on the main line, past the connector station, Grand Park exit, then up and over the river rapids to the terminus. Those heading for the "Middle East" change trains near the Akbar Café to take the northern spur. Here is where the whiter and darker ethnicities separate. The subway cars are new, clean, and smooth-running. In some, and in the station corridors, beggars and street musicians leave hats and instrument cases open for donations. Surprisingly, perhaps, the hands that drop the coins are more commonly dark than white, and in any case mostly local. Where the subway heads, tourists are unlikely to go unless it's to the Grand Park exit to visit the wooded areas of gardens and ponds and hordes of reportedly neutered cats (if neutered, why are there so many of them, one could ask). Small dog parks and informal soccer pitches are found in the park as well.

This, then, is today's Euroburg. Its long history takes it from a Roman outpost to slowly growing small town, accelerated in size and importance by the reach of the church, and then fully expanded by the commercial interests that forged the canal. New industries and the widening of the canal led to two cities, one old and one new. Pivotal events from the Black Death to the Second World War decimated the town, but successful reconstructions and waves of new residents forged a city of industrial and touristic merit. Now, as in much of Europe, the newest challenge of immigrant and refugee populations from the east and the Mediterranean rim has yet to reveal a 21st century urban style. But this much seems likely: street gangs, if they are to be found here, are likely to become a part of the style.

4. The Smokes

Memo To: Prof. Keller

From: Heinrich (Edited by Liz)

Date: July 24

Sir:

I apologize for missing a couple of seminar sessions, but as I told you I've been immersing myself in my investigation of the guys in Fort Araby. Liz has been with me on occasion, especially when talking to officials, but I don't like having her go into the projects. I think people will clam up in her presence, or maybe even exaggerate things, to impress her. She hates it when I say this, but I think gang ethnography is a man's world (Oh please! Editor Liz).

Fort Araby was constructed in the 1960s to house the new workers immigrating here mostly because of the new plants in the industrial area. I think this is important; the projects were built for workers, not for families (unlike the housing in "The Village" where family units were designed in). The projects are high story—four to eight floors—built close to each other and to the terminus of the subway, then also under construction. There's little there by way of playground or sports facilities, vegetable gardening areas, or offices for welfare or health officials. Schools, I was told, were an after-thought. The nearest shopping was in the underground areas of the subway station. But now Fort Araby has families—the workers didn't leave to go back to Turkey or Morocco or wherever, they just brought in their wives and kids (and a lot of uncles and cousins to boot). The result is terrible overcrowding, poor maintenance, and a lot of aimless people sitting around saying "What's up, man?" This is a lousy place, Professor. I don't understand why it hasn't been knocked down and replaced. Didn't you tell me that's what's been done in Chicago and Manchester?

I've talked with a bunch of agency people – welfare, school, building superintendents and the like, as well as some of the elders I've met at the Akbar Café. They think the worst problem is employment – actually, the lack of jobs, especially for the young people. Few jobs plus little local recreation plus ethnic segregation has led to lots of unconnected youths who have formed groups of one sort and another.

The group they talk about is the Smokes. It's the biggest youth group, they say up to 100 members, and causes the worst trouble. Most of them call the Smokes a gang because of the "trouble"- crimes and hassles with other groups. As far as I can make out, the crimes are not very serious. Lots of theft and vandalism (there's Smokes graffiti all over the place) and stuff they do downtown. I'm told the police don't like to go into the Fort – they're outnumbered and afraid, one of the elders told me.

I think there's not much serious violence; the same elder laughed and told me, "A threat a day keeps the cops away." He also said crime was not what started the Smokes. According to him, the Fort Araby kids were being "jumped" and robbed by some locals about 15 years ago. His description made me think of Skinheads. Anyway, the locals called the Fort kids "duskies" because of their darker skin, so these guys took on the name Duskies, recruited a few older cousins, and went back down and beat the shit out of the locals (please excuse his language: Editor Liz) and decided they were a "defensive club." The label Smokes was adopted later as being less negative (and according to a local welfare informant, because some of them started selling hashish). I don't know if this makes them a gang or not. Mustafa, a skinny little 15 year old, said "We're just a bunch of pals, y'know."

This Mustafa hardly strikes me as a gang member. He desperately wants to be accepted by the older Smokes and hangs around with them on the fringes, but some of the older guys reject him, say he has no balls (again, please excuse: Liz), and don't trust him. But because I listen to him, Mustafa tells me a lot about the Smokes. Even though he may exaggerate things, he's got his eyes open – and his mouth when he's with me.

Muhammed H. is just the opposite. He's 19 or 20 years old, a Smoke for over four years he says. When I asked him about the Smokes' criminal involvement, he confirms what others have said: they're into just about everything but not at serious levels. Most of the time, he says, they just "hang." I asked him about guns and weapons; he said "no guns—I have these, don't I?" (holding out his fists), "If someone gives me a stare, I just slap his face."

Kemal is another older teen – I'd guess 18 – who's been arrested several times. When I asked for what, he said "stealing from stores downtown, or from some dumb guy, like a watch or bomber jacket I like. But not here," he said, "always downtown because the subway is so easy. Stealing things can get you respect. You like my new cell phone?" I got the clear impression from these guys that they're not very territorial. If they have a turf, it's downtown. They commute to turf. Another guy told me about living in Fort Araby, "Nothing ever happens here. You have to go into town for something to do."

Some of what I know so far about the Smokes comes from guys like Kemal, and Muhammed, and Mustafa. Some of it comes from the elders in the Akbar. And some of it comes from agency people I talked to. They don't always agree on things, and my own time hanging around the area clarifies some things and makes me uncertain of others. But here are my impressions about the group as a whole.

There are maybe 50 to 100 actual members, and others seen occasionally who are either younger or older. Most are adolescent or up to 20 or 21. Some of the older guys in their 20s say they are still members but don't get involved. I don't know how to be sure what makes someone a gang member. Can we talk about this?

I don't find any clear leadership. In fact, the guys tell me things like "Nobody's the boss" (Aziz) and "Nobody is worth more than anyone else" (Khalid). There's a fairly clear younger group, ages 12 to 14 I'd guess, and Khalid seems to be very popular among them, but I don't see him telling them what to do. And among the older guys, Muhammed gets a lot of respect for the way he talks and Kemal's criminal activity gets him the respect he told me it does. Respect and influence seem important, but I'm not sure that makes these guys real leaders.

As you can see from the names, the Smokes are mostly Muslims, second and even third generations here. Some of them only speak a few Arabic words. The backgrounds are mostly Turkish and Moroccan plus a few from places like Kosovo and Bosnia. A couple of Euroburg kids are tolerated almost like mascots. Also, being Muslim, they don't allow girls to be members of the Smokes. There are girlfriends and sisters that I see during the day, but they're not part of the Smokes as far as I can tell. Mustafa says you can't trust girls, and their moms keep them at home anyway.

The other thing I can't get a good hold on is the group's cohesion. You said this was an important issue, but I'm not sure how to judge it. They're tight in the sense of claiming loyalty; Kemal was clear that "we don't snitch on each other" and coming to each other's aid is something everyone claims. But how can 100 guys be tight? How can they be cohesive with ages that go from twelve into the twenties, and when they seem to clique up separately by age or depending on which building they live in? Several agency officials have told me that street gangs are cohesive, but I just can't see it at this point, at least not among the Smokes.

I'm sorry to go on so long about all this, but I'm finding my foray into their world both intriguing and confusing. I need more time with them. And by the way, they've already given me a "street name": I'm Heinrich the Hound because I keep dogging them, hanging around, sniffing around. I get some of them to laugh now by barking at them! The down side to this is I've been asked a couple of times if I'm a nark (a drug cop) and my answer about being a student at the University doesn't seem very convincing. One older guy I don't know by name has the street name of "Samurai," maybe because of his Asian features. He told me, "Maybe you ask too many questions" and he wasn't smiling when he said it (Prof. Keller, can we talk about this, *please*: Editor Liz).

5. Background Statement: Street Gangs and other Youth Groups

[Special Comments from the Author]

Heinrich's difficulty in putting the label "gang" on the Smokes is a good sign. Many people use the label far too readily, while some others shy away from it for fear of stigmatizing youth groups. The term gang – in our case, "street gang" – deserves cautious use. It is a common feature of young people – pre-teens, teens, young adults – that they tend to form and join groups of their own age, their own kind. As youths, most of us were members of groups, but not of street gangs. We belonged to youth clubs, sports teams, school interest groups, social clubs, friendship cliques and the like. Many of these were sponsored by adults, but many were informal, unsupervised groups. Russian scholars have formalized the informal by adopting the term IFYs, or Informal Youth Groups.

   Individual members of such informal youth groups may on occasion commit delinquent acts. That certainly does not merit labeling the group a gang. Swedish scholar Jerzy Sarnecki has studied *networks* of delinquents, kids caught offending with each other, but Sarnecki wisely avoids referring to co-offenders or offender networks as street gangs. Since most youth commit one or more illegal acts at some point, and since many illegal acts are committed in the company of one of more other youth, co-offending is common. Street gangs are not.

Other youth groups come to be known for involvement in antisocial or illegal behavior, but yet do not achieve the status, in our terms, of street gang. In Europe, such groups having many forms have been studied by research scholars. In Russia, much has been written about Fanati (sports fan groups), Rokkeri (bikers), and Metallisti (heavy metal music fans). The Russians refer to these as groups with approved goals but illegal means. On occasion, such groups create very visible public nuisances in the pursuit of their interests. U.S. researchers have described taggers, bully gangs, party crews, stoners, punkers, and others. Zurich police have described "toy gangsters." Pitts in East London, Sanders in South London, Rus and Vigil in Chiapas, Mexico, Dekleva in Slovakia, Feixa in Barcelona, Schumann in Bremen, Kersten in Germany generally, Vercaigne in Brussels, and Gruter and Versteegh in the Hague have all reported on youth groups that could fit under a very broad umbrella of gang-like groups, yet we are hesitant to categorize them as genuine street gangs. Similarly, gang scholars (but not public officials) are reluctant to associate street gangs with prison gangs, terrorist gangs, motorcycle gangs, drug cartels, and other adult criminal enterprises.

Such a variety of groups creates considerable ambiguity, even conceptual conflict, when gang researchers come to the same table to discuss their work. Starting in 1997, such a group of researchers has been coming together in a series of workshops and meetings to foster a new enterprise, the development of cross-national comparative street gang research. Under the rubric of the Eurogang Program, up to 200 American and European gang experts have tackled various complex tasks, not the least of which was settling on a consensus definition of street gangs. Fully explicated in Klein and Maxson's *Street Gang Patterns and Policies* (Oxford, 2006) and illustrated in all the studies reported in Decker and Weerman's *European Street Gangs and Troublesome Youth Groups* (AltaMira, 2005), this definition overcomes the ambiguities and inconsistencies of a host of prior, uncoordinated approaches to gang definitions. It was designed by a working group of about 20 scholars from Europe and the U.S. It is simple yet comprehensive, applicable across countries so as to facilitate comparative conclusions about the nature of street gangs. The consensus Eurogang definition reads as follows:

> A street gang is any durable, street-oriented youth group whose involvement in illegal activity is part of its group identity.

Point 1: *Durable* is a bit ambiguous, but at least an existence of several months can be used as a guideline. Many gang-like groups come together and dissipate within a few months. The durability refers to the *group*, which continues despite turnover of members.

Point 2: *Street-oriented* implies spending a lot of group time outside home, work, and school—often on streets, in shopping malls, in parks, in cars, and so on.

Point 3: *Youth* can be ambiguous. Most street gangs are more adolescent than adult, but some include members in their 20s and even 30s. Most have average ages in adolescence or early 20s.

Point 4: *Illegal* generally means delinquent or criminal, not just bothersome.

Point 5: *Identity* refers to the group, not the individual self-image.

This minimalist definition of the street gang provides several points to consider. First, it requires only five defining factors: durability, street-orientation, youthfulness, group character, and illegal identity. These are the "definers." In contrast, most other gang definitions add items from a host of "descriptors," such as gender, ethnicity, colors and signs and clothing, group names, violent behavior, leadership, and so on. Given the Eurogang definition with the five definers, all these other characteristics can be used separately to compare gangs to each other, but none are required to define a group as a gang. Establishing the five "necessary and sufficient" requirements for gang definitions provides (1) a generic *class* of groups called street gangs, and (2) freedom to describe the many similarities and differences within that class.

Additionally, the Eurogang definition provides Heinrich and the rest of us with the means to distinguish between street gangs and most other groups sometimes labeled as gangs. Most youth groups do not fit the definition. Consider the earlier listings of the informal youth groups, the networks of co-offenders, and the troublesome groups such as rockers, stoners, and party crews. Most such youth groups are not street gangs and do not readily fit within the definers of the street gang.

Similarly, this street gang definition does not apply well to a host of more adult gangs that are often confused with street gangs. These would include, as noted, prison and terrorist and motorcycle gangs and drug cartels or criminal enterprises. These are certainly worth studying in their own right by criminologists and others, but separately from street gangs.

One final point can be made here. It is not uncommon, especially among those concerned with intervening in gang situations in order to reduce gang activity, to think of gangs as the extreme form of delinquency. Gangs, many feel, are merely collections of the worst offenders, those lying at the end of the severity continuum. Thus, it is assumed, practices useful in preventing or reducing delinquency generally can be applied as well to street gangs merely by increasing the intervention levels: more social service, more police enforcement or suppression, harsher judicial and correctional sanctions. This is reasonable but ultimately inappropriate thinking about gangs. It overlooks the kinds of processes that make street gangs not quantitatively but *qualitatively* different from other groups. Four features, in particular, make the gang a different phenomenon, not merely the end of the continuum.

1) Most, but certainly not all, street gang members come from marginalized populations. This refers primarily to ethnic, racial, or national minorities that result in socially excluded youth. Even among non-minority gangs, membership tends to be drawn from socially or economically marginalized youth (for example, many skinhead groups, the German "Aussiedlers" described by Weitekamp and the southern Italians in the north, described by Gatti). This marginalization feeds the gang's sense of being left out, hopeless and reliant on itself alone.

2) Street gangs come to identify themselves as criminally oriented (the identity definer) when they have reached and passed a "tipping point" of illegality. Their level of delinquent activity and orientation goes past that of other youth groups, calling forth condemnation from officials and community members and the self-recognition of the gang's special nature. Party crews, taggers, and other informal groups can be transformed into street gangs by passing the tipping point of criminal involvement to achieve this identity – just enough for it to become a salient definer.

3) Similarly, violence becomes a self definer of gang status. While most street gangs are not heavily involved in *acts* of violence, they do adopt the *rhetoric* of violence. They speak it, share it, exaggerate it, relish in it. Cops and gangs are alike in this respect at least; the "war stories" of confrontations are given salience well beyond the merits of the violent incidents. The repeated rhetoric of violence adds a measure of cohesiveness to the group that goes well beyond the common bonds of marginalization and joint leisure activities. No matter the actual level of violence in a street gang, one *hears* much of it.

4) Finally, as a result of these three and other factors, street gangs develop what Moore and Vigil have labeled an "oppositional culture." This refers to both individual and group processes that allow gang members to turn external interventions into group solidifiers. The special, supportive moves of street workers become signals to the gang of its special nature. The extra surveillance or suppression by the police feeds the cohesiveness of the gang by providing an "enemy" on which the group depends. The additional sanctions of the court, the exclusion of gang members from regular schools and job opportunities, the disdain of community members and age peers all are taken to prove the unfairness of the surrounding society which must therefore be

resisted. Whether the intentions of others are positive or negative, they are transmuted by the gang into oppositional forces that serve to increase gang cohesiveness. For well-intentioned persons hoping to prevent, intervene with, and control activity, the effect of this oppositional culture is to defeat their purposes – automatically – by a group that can and will turn the positive into a negative. For those who would mount anti-gang programs, this transmuting process may raise the most daunting challenge of all: how to effect positive change that is not turned upside down by the targets of change.

6. The Team Gathers

July 31 witnessed two changes in Euroburg, the first massive and habitual, the second hardly noticeable yet unique. The first was the emptying of Euroburg or, more accurately, the flight of Euroburgers to the south, to vacations in Greece, Southern Italy and Sicily, to Spain's Gold Coast and other collections of seaside timeshares, resorts, and second homes. Left in town were the tourists in their peak season and the locals who serviced them.

The "hardly noticeable" change was the transformation of Prof. Keller's seminar group into his research team. The group gathered for the last session, not in the seminar room but in Keller's conference room at the Criminology Institute. As in many post-war European cities, the university had consisted of numerous institutes, schools, and departments located where they originated throughout the town. The "central campus", for the most part, simply didn't exist.

But with reconstruction, urban expansion, and major increases in student enrollments, various components of the university were shifted from their old housing to more centralized locations – the north campus and the south campus (still no lawns, but many connecting walkways). A few institutes were still left in their old sites, usually because of low prestige or convenience of location. The criminology institute was one of these, within walking distance of the old courthouse and the shiny new police station near the eastern canal bridge and the rail yards.

The building was 17th century, restored except for a few symbolic shrapnel wounds remaining from the bombing of the rail yards. Its typical limestone and wood façade featured murals on the outside of early scholars dispensing wisdom to eager students admiring them from below. But one did not find such themes repeated inside the building. The interior was modern, sterile, full of bulletin boards and plaster-board walls and noisy hallways. Whoever had been in charge of furnishing Prof. Keller's conference room on the second floor – his assistant, Magda, was usually blamed – had taken the issue to its extreme. The entire collection of tables, chairs, cabinets, bookcases, even white boards, was from Ikea – bland, Finnish ash with bright colored splashes of cloth and trimming. Old Euroburg had been banished from criminology.

In the room on this day, the last of the seminars and the first of the new research team, sat a small but diverse group. Keller was slender, in his early fifties, with the first signs of salt and pepper hair needing a barber's attention. The pipe was almost always in his mouth or hand but unlit. Both his wife and Magda had banned matches and lighters from his presence. Keller wore suit and tie; he always wore suit and tie as was expected of a university professor. His students addressed him as "Professor Keller", never by his first name.

Heinrich and Liz were there, the smaller "Hein" in wrinkled street clothes and the taller Liz in formal summer wear that bespoke her outgoing nature. Conrad and Dirk, the seminar students who had also opted for the street gang topic, sat opposite Hein and Liz. They were younger and new to the mysteries of crime, attentive non-contributors to the earlier discussions.

At the other end of the conference table from Keller sat Magda with her laptop computer at her fingertips, like a piano to its master. To think of Magda without her laptop was as odd as imagining Keller without his pipe. In her late 30s, Magda was as unremarkable in appearance as she was efficient as Keller's assistant. As the gang research progressed, she would keep in touch with all that happened, and make much of it happen as well. She would be, with her laptop, the recorder of all issues and discussions, supervisor of field observers and interview coders. She would be at one time the disciplinarian and at others the mother bear to the students and field workers. She proved that one can be equally obsessive and supportive. Keller was the conceptual center of the team; it was Magda who made it a team.

Keller opened the discussion by confirming their status; The Mayor's office had transferred funds to the university contracts office to support a full year, if not more, of a "comprehensive study" of youth group problems in Euroburg, whatever that meant. Keller would define that for them, but first he asked Heinrich for a brief summary of what he and Liz had learned about the Smokes because, as Keller put it, "I want it to be clear at this point that what we have is not just a youth group study, but a street gang study."

"Well," Heinrich started, "they're all out of Fort Araby, and you all know what that means – you've seen my memo to Professor Keller. There may be as many as a hundred, mostly teens, who claim to be Smokes. It's almost all Muslim guys, but they're mostly born and raised here. They don't like the Fort, but pretty much live there anyway. But they don't mess up there…they come into town on the subway to spend a lot of their time, and its here in town that they get into trouble – not big trouble, mostly, but lots of stealing and smash-and-grab stuff, and the tagging and graffiti you can see around the station and Old Town. I've got a few good contacts already – guys named Mustafa, and Muhammed, and Kemal, and some elders at the Akbar Café. Liz talked to some elders too. I get the sense that respect and status are what they're really all about – they don't get much from Euroburgers so they stress it among themselves. There's a lot of anger, too. Also, there seem to be some other groups we may want to study if there's enough money. There's a group in the "Village" called the Zealots, and we've seen skinheads on some occasions, and two agency workers said there's another group some businessmen call a gang in the Backwater area."

Liz quickly chimed in: "There's more. Just because these are Muslim guys doesn't mean there aren't any Smokes girls. I've seen several hanging together who said they'd talk to me if I wanted. I think Hein is just as sexist as the Smokes boys. And the other thing is that I think Hein has to cool it a bit. He thinks he can just walk in and gain rapport despite his different background. I worry that he's wrong. He's already gotten one clear threat. I think we should be very careful out there – I may be safer as a woman than Hein or Dirk or Conrad are."

Magda's laptop had been clicking away through all this, but it stopped as she reached over to put her hand on Liz's arm. Keller then addressed them all, in his quiet professional fashion, taking them along his road from being his students to being his researchers. First he emphasized the ethical issues, researchers intruding into other people's private and cultural worlds. This requires respect for them at all times. "We are information gatherers, not social practitioners. We count on their trust in us, but we have to build this trust by being as non-judgmental as we can. But we can't condone illegal activity; if we are clear about this, they'll understand and keep us in a neutral status."

He also told them that every field observer and interviewer would have to fill out a waiver form, at the university's assistance, that stated (1) the researcher would do nothing to endanger or compromise a research subject's privacy rights, (2) the researcher would engage in no illegal activity, and (3) the researcher would not hold the university liable for any criminal injury sustained in the process of doing the research. Magda would get these forms from the legal counsel and have them signed and filed. "And," she said, "pay attention to what Liz said. Don't overstep your bounds. Don't challenge these people you're studying. I'm not a trained nurse." Liz looked at her gratefully.

Keller then moved on to stress putting what was learned in Euroburg into the much larger context of street gangs in Europe and America as well – the latter because that's where the bulk of the research had been done. He talked about particularly interesting studies in Europe that team members should read, such as Patrick's study in Glasgow, Werdmulder's in Amsterdam, and the many articles in the two books from the Eurogang Program. "We want to understand our Euroburg gangs as they exist *here* – if indeed they do – but we must not let this blind us to their place in the larger universe of street gangs. There is much in common across gangs in other places."

Keller continued with several points:

1. Street gangs are, first and foremost, *groups*. Group processes of cohesiveness, group norms, leadership, in-group and out-group feelings and so on force a certain amount of sameness across gangs that trumps differences in ethnicity, gender, community, and geographic factors.

2. Street gangs generally occur in the contexts of racism, poverty, lowered opportunities, and inadequate resources. The members tend to consist of socially excluded youth, whether Pakistanis in Oslo, Turks in Berlin or Zurich, Moroccans in Holland or Belgium, "Yardies" in London, or blacks and Hispanics in the U.S. The urban segregated context forces common bonds among affected youth. It is not the particular ethnic or national grouping that is at issue; it's the marginalization and sense of social exclusion that is important. For instance, an interesting review of Dutch gangs undertaken by Frank van Gemert reveals a progression in gang ethnicities that mirrors waves of immigrations in that country over four decades: from Surinamese to Moroccan to Antillean. Gangs derive from communities.

3. Youth drawn to street gangs are for the most part the less successful youth within their own neighborhoods. They are the minority within the minority. Their common social inadequacies yield a further sharing of characteristics that separates them from the other youth in the same communities who do not join with them.

4. Forget the stereotypic images of Westside Story, or the storied American groups like the Crips and Bloods, the Latin Kings and prison gangs. Most street gangs are more like caricatures of normal youth groups, with the added dimension of antisocial orientation. Research derived from American studies but shown to apply in Europe as well has revealed a typology of five gang structures that encompasses most street gangs fairly well. This typology allows us to see beyond the "one size fits all" or "all gangs are alike" mentality and

recognize *patterns* of similarities. This is how knowledge is built, by finding patterns, and their meaningful individual differences. "I will be surprised," said Keller, "if our Euroburg groups or gangs do not fit within these patterns already described in the gang literature. For instance, Heinrich's description of the Smokes seems to fit one of the five types, known as Neo-traditional gangs. We'll see, as we continue to collect the kind of data that relate to gang structures."

5. The whole idea of a research team implies a common goal as well as different skills and interests. Our common goal is to build knowledge about the street gangs of Euroburg, keeping in mind how that fits with more universal gang knowledge as well as the interests of our concerned citizens and authorities here in the city. But the team members will have preferences in styles and differences in research approaches. "Loyalty must not be to the individual approaches, or to me or Magda, or the Mayor. Loyalty has to be to the project and its goal. I'm going to keep stressing this. Magda, I trust, is the glue that will hold it all together." She stopped clicking for a moment.

He glanced up at her. He asked if there were any questions, but then proceeded as if he had not asked. "One last thing," he continued, "if I had been asked to take on this project without some very important help, I would have said no. But I knew help was there, and it's what will make the project possible. I'm talking about the Eurogang Program of course, which we discussed in the seminar. From this day on, we're going to be a small part of that program. Magda will see to it that our names are added to the Eurogang listserv run by Prof. Kerner at The University of Tubingen. There are over 150 names of researchers already on that list, both European and American. We will have access to all their research instruments developed, pilot-tested, and translated in half a dozen countries. The book edited by Decker and Weerman reports on a number of studies using those instruments. We will use them as well.

"Meanwhile, ever since the meeting of the mayor's panel, Magda has been compiling a list of studies of European gangs carried out by Eurogang Program researchers. She found these mostly in the listing in the University of Tubingen criminology library and on the internet. She gave me her notes yesterday evening and here's what is available to all of us to start reviewing:

Experts Surveys: seven articles on studies in six countries;
Youth Interviews: fifteen articles on studies in nine countries;
Ethnographic Guidelines: eight articles on studies in six countries;
News Reports: four articles on studies in four countries;
Archival Data: five articles on studies in four countries.

"Most, but not all of those studies were conducted in the early days of the Eurogang Program. As such, they used different variations of the data sources. We will have the advantage of using the final version of each Eurogang instrument, each one employing the consensus Eurogang definition of a street gang. We will have more continuity than has been possible in most of these other research projects," he said pridefully.

While Magda lists the Eurogang instruments on the board, I'll pass out to you copies of the Eurogang's Use Form that I've already filled in. Also, there is a website for the program <www.umsl.edu/~cci/eurogang/euroganghome. htm>. You can access it and get all the material there. Magda has copies in her office. Meanwhile, we'll leave the list on the board:"

1. Experts Survey
2. Youth Survey
3. Ethnographic Guidelines
4. City Descriptors
5. Gang Intervention Survey

"One matter not listed there is a procedure for extracting data from police reports. We'll have to talk about that issue fairly soon."

Heinrich couldn't let that one go. "Sir, you made it clear in the seminar that the police don't record a lot of stuff about gangs and gang crime, and we know how they exaggerate. Why should we bother getting police data?"

"Because they have it, and we don't," Keller replied. "Don't worry, we'll talk more about this. Any other questions?" he asked as he gathered his papers and prepared to leave without expecting any further discussion. The team leader had led. It was time to go home to his scotch and his wife. And he did, but the four students remained, as did Magda. She would thrust and parry with them for another hour – it was another of her functions for the Professor. Then the four left for beers down the street, and Magda went home to her partner for wine and Euroburger sausages, a local delicacy.

Malcolm W. Klein

Use of Eurogang Program Instruments

Investigators are invited to use the instruments developed by the Eurogang Program, including: the definition of "street gang", the youth or school survey, the experts survey, ethnographic guidelines and summary sheet, city level data compilation guidelines, and the prevention/ intervention inventory. Instruments will be provided one at a time, through the procedure described below. The goal of the Eurogang Program is to promote comparative research through multi-method, multi-site research. Key to the Eurogang program is the use of the accepted definition of a gang as "ANY DURABLE, STREET-ORIENTED YOUTH GROUP WHOSE INVOLVEMENT IN ILLEGAL ACTIVITY IS PART OF THEIR GROUP IDENTITY."

The Eurogang instruments represent a multinational, collaborative development and pre-testing initiative conducted since 1998. The instruments collect key information designated by Eurogang as critical to describing and understanding the groups of interest, and we encourage use of instruments in their entirety. Changes in item order, wording or substantial meaning, or the omission of core items, place our goal of the collection of comparative, multi-method, cross-national information at risk.

For those wishing to use any of the instruments, we have the following conditions:

- We ask that you submit the attached form identifying yourself and describing the research purpose for which you will be using the instrument(s) to Cheryl Maxson (cmaxson@uci.edu).
- You communicate with a member of the Eurogang Program so that we can be informed about design advancements. The facilitator of each working group (see individual instrument protocol description below) is the preferred contact for individual instrument design questions and to share your experience with use.
- If you make a new translation, you send a copy of the new translation to the instrument working group facilitator to be available to others needing a version in your language (you will be identified as the source of the translation).
- Presentations and written reports should acknowledge the instruments with: "Instruments developed by the Eurogang Research Program." Please make sure that your Eurogang contact has a copy of any reports

30

or publications resulting from your use of the instruments; with your permission, these may be posted on the Eurogang website.

- These instruments have been developed in collaboration with researchers from many countries. They collect key information designated by Eurogang as critical to describing and understanding the groups of interest. Changes in item order, wording or substantial meaning, or the omission of items, place our goal of the collection of comparative, multi-method, cross-national information at risk. If you find it necessary to delete or otherwise change items offered in the instruments, please inform us of any changes you make. We appreciate your efforts to document alterations in these original instruments. We expect that items of special interest to individual researchers may be added.

Eurogang Instrument Working Group Facilitators: Definitions guidelines: Malcolm Klein mklein@usc.edu;City-level data: Elmar Weitekamp elmar. weitekamp@uni-tuebingen.de; Expert informant survey: Cheryl Maxson maxson@uci.edu; Youth/school/community survey: Finn Esbensen esbensen@umsl.edu; Ethnography: Jody Miller jodymiller@umsl.edu; Prevention/intervention: Scott Decker deckers@msx.umsl.edu

Eurogang Steering Committee: Juanjo Medina juanjo. medina@manchester.ac.uk, Finn Esbensen esbensen@umsl.edu, Frank van Gemert f.vangemert@rechten.vu.nl, Cheryl Maxson cmaxson@uci. edu, Frank Weerman Weerman@nscr.nl

Malcolm W. Klein

Request for Use of Eurogang Instruments

Your name: _____

Affiliation and address:

_____

_____

_____

_____

_____

Phone: _____ Fax: _____ Email: _____

Name of Eurogang contact(s):

_____

_____

Instrument(s) that you wish to use:

_____

_____

_____

_____

_____

Description of intended use of instrument(s):

_____

_____

_____

_____

_____

_____

_____

_____

To be completed by person providing the instruments:

Name of instrument: _____ Date: _____

Provided by: _____

Rev. 5/21/05

7. Teams Have Members

It was August, so as quickly as the initial team was confirmed, its members dispersed to various locales. Magda and her partner headed for Greece, as her parents had before her for many years. An isolated hotel on the island of Skiathos provided a pool above the sea, and sandy beaches ranging from the most sedate to the well known nude variety.

Magda's "partner" – the term she always used – was unknown and unseen by team members. Even the partner's gender was unknown, and therefore the target of much speculation. No one dared ask, but once, during a more informal discussion of families, Keller asked, "May I ask you a personal question?"

"No" was the simple and firm reply. He never asked again, and never felt any need to. Magda was his right hand, and often more, not to be poked and queried for his satisfaction. What plays with Magda stays with Magda. She treats him with the same respect, although students sometimes snicker at what they call his "dinosaur" status. He does not use the computer, he does not do emails. Magda handles all this for him. Overhearing the term "dinosaur" on one occasion, he responded to Liz, "No, I'm a self-made Eurosaur, an endangered species requiring environmental protection." He never heard "dinosaur" again.

Liz and Heinrich did not leave town in August. They were tethered to Euroburg, the university, and each other. Their styles were complementary, sometimes with a little tension because of her role as his "handler." She was a feminist, where he exuded masculinity. She was enthusiastic, even vibrant with a clothing style both neat and colorful. He dressed "informally" in his view, sloppily as others saw it. He was a sloucher in tie-dyed t-shirts with leftist slogans (George Bush and Margaret Thatcher did not fare well on Heinrich's chest). He was the quiet one, unless crossed or aroused by moral issues. Even their research stylistic preferences were at odds. She was a survey researcher with strong statistical skills. She used words like reliability and validity as synonymous with truth. Heinrich was the field observer, the interviewer, an ethnographer at heart if not by strict training. He believed in "grounded theory" and eschewed representative sampling as if it distorted the reality of a good case study. It would be for Magda and Keller to marry these styles, if not these students. It was the structure of the Eurogang Program that would make this possible on Keller's gang project.

Heinrich and Liz knew their place during August was in town, poking around. Gang members usually don't take summer vacations. In cities, they become more active criminally because of the influx of tourists. Hein would hang out in Old Town and around the train station in the evenings. Liz wanted to get a better view of the girls, whether around Fort Araby or in town. And, she needed to delve into the empirical literature on girls in street gangs.

Dirk and Conrad had a different approach. Both were new to the Free University and to Euroburg. They had enrolled there specifically because of Prof. Keller's international reputation in criminal law, criminal behavior, and research methods in criminology. Dirk came from Holland, Conrad from Sweden. Neither yet felt much at home in Euroburg, so both returned home to their families in August and thence to the Gold Coast for two weeks. But they would learn that to be Keller's students meant they would be "on call," in their case returning home to meet with him, Dirk in Amsterdam and Conrad in Stockholm. Keller was on the move.

For Martin Keller, this August "vacation" presented a special opportunity. Now in his mid-fifties, he is no longer intrigued by doing direct field research. He's had enough days in the rain, in the dark, in jails and prisons, in the musty file rooms, enough cruising the streets in police ride-alongs and sitting in courtrooms watching the tediously slow process of justice staggering along. Still, Keller is a respected criminologist with a strong bent towards empirical studies that can be replicated in multiple settings. This makes the Eurogang Program highly relevant for him. He believes in shared data and is suspicious of other researchers' "insights, intuitions, and private knowledge," as he puts it.

Importantly, he is a frequent traveler who enjoys contacts with foreign colleagues. Unlike many of his colleagues, he chose to study for his PhD. in America, starting at the University of Albany and finishing at the University of Pennsylvania with masters like Thornton Sellin and Marvin Wolfgang. With this, and visiting positions at the Universities of Leiden and Uppsala as well as the Max Planck Institute in Freiburg, he was a shoo-in for the sole criminology professorship at the Free University of Euroburg. He settled there with his artist wife and raised two girls, now beyond school and creating their own new worlds.

Keller's wife is a crafts artist, with emphasis on woven goods and ceramics. Their home is full of hangings on the walls, woolen runners on the tables and ceramic miniatures scattered about. With their children gone, her thought was to open her own crafts shop in Old Town. It would include her own work, local crafts from the surrounding area, but also imports from around Europe. It was this thought plus her husband's interest in other Eurogang research sites that, in short course, formed their August vacation. They would visit Eurogang sites for him to contact gang research colleagues while she scouted the crafts scenes.

They started in Tubingen, Germany, where Keller's long-time colleague Prof. Hans-Jurgen Kerner had amassed an extensive criminological library and also maintained a Eurogang listserv of almost 200 researchers. While Mrs. Keller scouted Black Forest crafts, -- cuckoo clocks, miniature ceramic trolls, and delicate painted glass bells seemed most promising -- the two professors chose five sites where a variety of gangs had been reported. While Kerner contacted researchers in each site, Keller sat down with one of them, Tubingen's Elmar Weitekamp, and learned about local gangs of "Aussiedlers." These were eastern Europeans, mostly Russian-based immigrants whose parents or grandparents had been German. With the fall of the Berlin Wall, a rush of these immigrants was flooding Germany. By German law, they were German citizens, yet they spoke no German and retained nothing of German culture. They were eastern Europeans in their own foreign land, doubly marginalized and largely rejected by indigenous German society. Weitekamp briefly described how their own more violence-tolerant upbringing and social exclusion in newly unified Germany had fostered Ausseidler gangs, even in Tubingen, a primarily university town. This seemed an interesting contrast to the Smokes of Euroburg.

In turn, the Kellers' travel sites by train and plane were Stockholm, Oslo, Amsterdam, and Genoa. In Stockholm, they were met by Conrad who steered

Mrs. Keller to two lovely craft shops, one on the main street, Sveavagen, and the other up the hill in Gamla Stan, Stockholm's Old Town (though not so old as in most other cities). The prizes were glassware by Kosta Boda and Orrefors, woven goods, birch plates and utensils, and beautifully carved Sami (Lapplander) jewelry from reindeer horns and bone.

For Keller, Stockholm produced conflicting stories. Professor Jerzy Sarnecki described his research on delinquent networks, youth arrested as co-offenders by the police. None of these co-offending networks could be equated with street gangs. Indeed, Sarnecki insisted that there were no such gangs in Stockholm. Yet Conrad had scouted up a young anthropologist actively engaged in ethnography of a Stockholm gang. Further visits to the central police station yielded a police officer who had diagrammed youth networks on her wall, complete with mug shot photos of each youth.

"Are these really gangs?" asked Keller and Conrad in unison. As an answer, she (the officer) took them on an evening tour through downtown and the underground area of Sergelstorg in the center of the city. Sure enough, there were clusters of mostly Turkish youth loitering about, smoking hash and hassling local shoppers. For Keller's sake, she asked them where they were from. The answer was Rinkeby, a housing development on the outskirts of town, connected directly to downtown by the subway. The officer knew almost all of them, their street names, and as she put it, their "criminal gang names." Keller and Conrad easily saw the parallel to Euroburg.

Next came Oslo, with wool sweaters and Nordic wall hangings for Mrs. Keller. A trio of gang researchers had responded to Hans-Jurgen Kerner's request. Toré Bjorgo described local skinhead gangs, and Ingve Carlsson spoke about special, community-based programs to deal with them. Inger-Lise Lien described some gangs composed of indigenous Norwegian youth and others of Pakistani immigrants. Her data on the latter, she pointed out, revealed very strong familial patterns of gang membership, far more extensive, she said, than reported for street gangs anywhere else. "And," she said, "they don't necessarily gather in public places. It gets too cold in Norway to do that. But they're in constant communication with each other and can be called together quickly if the need arises." Gang members of this new era are cohesive via cell phones, another lesson for Keller and Conrad to take home with them.

The fourth site was Amsterdam, and Dirk's turn to join Keller while his wife concentrated on antique jewelry and porcelains, especially Delft tiles. Keller and Dirk toured the canals on a small boat steered by Frank van Gemert of The Free University of Amsterdam. Van Gemert's ethnographic work had been primarily with Moroccan gang members in Amsterdam. He was leery of comparing them to other ethnic groups and to American gangs for several reasons. Their origins in the Rif mountainous region of Northern Morocco included strong tribal hostilities and suspicions leaving them less likely to form cohesive or well-structured gangs. They also seemed non-territorial in Amsterdam and therefore had not formed intergang rivalries. Rather, conflicts arise with local shopkeepers and neighborhood residents. The canal trip was touristic – the gang boys, as in Euroburg, lived in housing developments away from the center of the city. Finally, an item that intrigued Keller, in particular, was the collaboration that van Gemert has established with an American gang ethnographer, Mark Fleisher. They were working the Amsterdam scene together as a result of their mutual participation in the Eurogang Program. For Keller, this triggered some new thoughts about his American contacts as sources of help in Euroburg.

The final stop in the August vacation was Genoa. The contact there was another of Keller's old-time colleagues, Uberto Gatti. While Mrs. Keller checked on local decorative gold, silver, and ceramic arts, her husband found several surprises. Gatti had originally questioned the premises of the Eurogang Program and its depiction of the gang situation. This skepticism, however, was altered radically when Gatti found two, contrasting gang problems within his own city. The first of these was (yet again) a separated housing project encompassing Southern Italian "immigrants" from Calabria and Sicily. Unconnected to the better known adult or Mafia group, these gang members from the far south felt as marginalized in Genoa way up north as did immigrants from distant shores. They were isolated and excluded from mainstream Genoa youth and families. The parallel to Germany's Ausseidlers did not escape Professor Keller.

The second gang development was among Latino immigrants, primarily from Ecuador. Information on these youth was sketchy, as the police were not yet clear on distinctions between youth groups and street gangs, but Gatti reported that similar Latino gang problems were being newly reported in Barcelona and Madrid. And while the language and cultural connections to Spain made sense, why such immigration to Genoa was taking place was not clear. Nonetheless, Gatti was preparing to add Latino gang research to his study of the Southern Italian groups.

So the August vacation was very useful. Mrs. Keller was confirmed in her desire to start a Euroburg crafts shop and knew that a wide variety of goods could be available. Her husband, in turn, had a new appreciation for the variety of European gang situations which could serve as a context for his team's work in Euroburg and for assuring officials there that they were not alone or unique in facing a street gang problem.

On returning to the office, he found two research papers by Joachim Kersten in Germany, sent on by Hans-Jurgen Kerner. Both were descriptions of a wide range of German youth groups that were *not* street gangs, yet were troublesome youth phenomena nonetheless. The distinctions between such groups and street gangs as defined in the Eurogang Program would be worth presenting to his team members as another context for considering the nature of the street gangs in Euroburg.

8. Girls in Street Gangs

For Liz, August did not provide the level of satisfaction achieved by her professor. She had hoped to learn about girls in gangs, especially female Smokes. How many were there, why did they join, what did they get from their membership, what sorts of crime did they commit? At first, Liz thought she saw a number of girl Smokes, but pressed by Hein's skepticism about her questions, she began to have doubts.

To be the girlfriend of a gang member, she found, need not mean being a gang member. Sisters and close cousins, too, may hang with the Smokes on occasion, further confusing the issue. Heinrich asked her pointedly about her observed girls, "Do they hang with the boys over several months, in public places, thinking of themselves as being in a criminally involved, group?" He was attacking her with the consensus Eurogang definition they had both learned from Martin Keller.

Liz couldn't respond well to Heinrich's attack. She couldn't get close enough to the girls she observed, nor to the boys. She tried to learn from the elders at the Akbar Café, but was shunned there. One said to her directly, "We tolerate your presence outside the bar because of your friend, but don't push us; you're a woman, and not one of us." The best she could learn, from comments here and there, was that Muslim girls should not be seen with boys, although in other gangs they might. Other gangs? She would have to report such comments to Prof. Keller.

If field research was unrewarding, maybe the library could yield what Liz needed. As soon as the summer seminar had started, Magda had enlisted the aid of the university library in accumulating street gang studies throughout Europe. The search was wide but did not yield a large number of works. Much of it was found in the two books produced by the Eurogang Program. Other studies existed but revealed few patterns. Liz found little to help her.

There were brief mentions of girls affiliated with gangs in Oslo and Luzern, and of autonomous girl gangs in Duisberg and Madrid. A 2006 summary article on street gang violence suggested that there was little mention of girls in European gangs, perhaps the authors suggested because much of that research was on Muslim gangs of Algerian, Moroccan, Turkish, and Pakistani derivations.

Liz was not about to report such a limited story to the research team. There had to be more, so she widened her library search to include non-European, mostly American studies. Here, she found much more, although how well it might apply to Euroburg was unclear. She organized her material under a number of brief headings for presentation in September.

1. Street gangs typically *do* include female members. Police data generally suggested from zero to five percent female prevalence, but this seemed to be a major under count. American police pay little attention to girls; surveys and ethnographies, by contrast, find female participation to be between 20 and 50 percent depending on the city and the ages of gang members studied. Surely the team would have to stay alert to the girls in Euroburg.

2. Three forms of female participation were described. Autonomous girl gangs are quite rare, perhaps accounting for five to ten percent of all cases. More common were female auxiliary groups (Latin Queens with Latin Kings, Cripettes with Crips, and so on) estimated to account for roughly a third of female gang members. More than half of the girls fell into the third category belonging to more integrated, mixed-gender gangs. In each case, the studies suggested, female membership was more than originally suggested as just a matter of girls carrying weapons or drugs for the boys, or being there only for sexual exploitation – "toys for boys." In each of the three forms, females were genuine members in their own rights.

3. Female gang members, on the whole, tended to be younger than the males, and with lower status. This might help explain why the police were less aware of and interested in them than were gang researchers.

4. Reasons for girls joining gangs in many ways parallel those for boys, but with more emphasis on reactions to serious family problems and amorous relationships to the boys.

5. Illegal behaviors among the girls were generally at a lower level than among the boys, although higher nonetheless than many non-gang boys. These girls deserved more police attention than the police themselves recognized. In many cases female members were excluded by male members from participation in criminal incidents, through male chauvinism and the boys' concern that girls would "fink"—tell on them to the police.

Three additional findings intrigued Liz the most. First, even though the girls' crime levels were lower, their crime "profiles" resembled that of the boys. That is, they showed the same ratios of minor (most common) to moderate to serious (least common) crimes. Girl gang members did not seem to specialize in gender-specific crimes; what the boys did, they also did although at lower levels.

Second, gang crime levels were in part a function of the gender ratio in a gang. Mixed gender gangs committed more crime than either predominantly male or predominantly female gangs. Gender structure, Liz was pleased to include in her feminist approach, needed to be included in the list of gang structure variables along with age, size, leadership, and the like.

Finally, to be a female member of any but autonomous female gangs was to be exposed to extra rates of victimization. This includes sexual assault, of course, but also various forms of non-sexual assault, mostly at the hands of male gang members. Female gang participation, Liz learned, brings extra danger. And of course, it brings potentially serious consequences for young adulthood, including drug addictions and marital problems. If these American findings were relevant to European – and Euroburg – gang girls, then the Professor's research team would have to pay heed and not assume that street gangs are "merely" a masculine problem. For the remainder of Keller's research project, Liz would be the team's reminder: "Don't forget the girls."

9. The Consultant

My dear friend:

I hope this letter finds you well as summer dims, and fully enjoying your retirement. I hesitate to disturb your well-earned peace, but I am inspired by my recent trip to engage your interest in my new project. I visited several countries and met with some of your Eurogang colleagues, all of whom suggested that I contact you. I should have done so earlier.

When last we met, at the A.S.C. convention in Los Angeles, you talked briefly about the Eurogang Program and inquired of my interest in street gang research. I had little, then, but things have changed. My purpose now is to reverse the situation and seek out your involvement – or, as my administrative assistant Magda put it, I should seduce you with "desires and dollars."

Three months ago, news reports of youthful or gang violence caught the attention of our citizens and public officials here in Euroburg. A minor "moral panic" seemed to bloom, but was stalled by our clever mayor who called a public hearing on the issue and then followed that up with the securing of funds – a rather generous amount, I must say – to support a thorough research investigation into the status of gang crime in our city. Does it really exist and, if so, what is its nature and what should the city do in response to it?

Malcolm W. Klein

The research funds were assigned to The Free University's Criminology Institute and more specifically to yours truly. I agreed to take on the project, initiated discussions among students in my summer seminar, and have brought together a research team which may be expanded. At the moment, it consists of myself, the marvelous Magda, and four graduate students of whom two are more experienced and two are quite new. Three points about our initial steps are worth mention at this point.

1. We have identified one large street gang of middle-eastern heritage and probably a second, rival group. One or two others have been mentioned to us (including skinheads) but we have no confirmation on these.

2. We have committed ourselves to using the Eurogang definition of street gangs, and to gathering data using the Eurogang Program's several instruments. I suppose a more accurate statement would be that I have committed us to these.

3. I have visited with some of your European colleagues (in two cases with the newer students) to understand better what we may be facing and to understand better some of the research issues. These colleagues have included my old friends Hans-Jurgen Kerner and Uberto Gatti, but also Elmar Weitekamp, Jerzy Sarnecki, Inger-Lise Lien, Toré Björgo, and Frank van Gemert. I must say, you have chosen well – charming and knowledgeable scholars, all. They each mentioned your role in initiating the program, one of them referring to you as their "silverback."

My memory of you is not quite that apian, but the reference seemed complimentary. So, I would like to engage you as a project consultant, to meet with us soon and often here in Euroburg and help us apply the program to our local situations. If my funds are low, the deputy mayor has assured me that his office will provide consultant funds, although he also mentioned that seeing your picture and story in the Euroburg Daily News would seem appropriate in return. The gang issue will be politically "hot" here for some time, and there is a news reporter who is following the issue quite closely (with an unfortunate tendency toward hyperbole).

How could you help us? Certainly you will have your own thoughts on this, but at least initially I have some suggestions. You could bring us up to date on relevant gang literature. I'm trying to familiarize myself with recent European studies, but your acquaintance with the far more extensive American research would be valuable. You could suggest research directions and obstacles for us to consider, and what staffing additions might make for an effective research team. You could fill in some gaps in our familiarity with the Eurogang Program. For example:

How do American and European gang situations compare (i.e., your "Eurogang Paradox")?

How do the research instruments hold up across countries?

Are there particular kinds of gangs we should be aware of? I have seen reference to your Maxson/Klein gang typology.

How do different types of gangs relate to programs to control them?

What kinds of control programs – prevention or intervention or legal and penal – seem to be promising, and what kinds might you describe to us already existing in Europe?

What kinds of research approaches might we consider beyond those seen in the several Eurogang Program instruments?

Well, that's enough questions for now – enough I hope to meet Magda's notions for your "seduction." I don't have any idea what your schedule is like, nor whether you are continuing your involvement in gang matters. But if on the basis of all this the Euroburg street gang project would be of interest to you, please let me hear from you. I am excited about our prospects and would enjoy your participation.

Your colleague and friend

Martin S. Keller

P.S. Should you agree to visit us, I would be pleased to tour you about Euroburg, and also have my students take you into their gang territories if that is your wish.

To: Martin S. Keller <mkeller@fue.edu>

I received your fascinating personal letter and invitation. I trust an e-mail response is appropriate. I have no hesitancy in accepting your offer. The project sounds like an intriguing challenge, and visits to European cities are one of my retirement pleasures (I often travel with my wife – be forewarned). The questions you pose are certainly appropriate and I will enjoy discussing these issues with you and your students. I'll also recommend a few items for them to read, but I assume the two Eurogang books are already in your Institute library. In return, I'll want to hear from them what they have learned about the Euroburg street gangs and how well they do or don't fit into the Maxson/Klein typology.

Incidentally, in May of 2008, we will be holding the ninth Eurogang Workshop – EG IX – which among other things is designed to expose more American young scholars to the program and to entice them (or seduce them in your Magda's term) to carry out comparative gang research with European colleagues such as those you listed in your letter. It occurs to me, of course, that engaging one or two American graduate students with those on your team could be a very nice consequence of our collaboration. I trust your students speak English reasonably well; our American students tend to monolingualism.

In any case, yes, your offer is accepted. As soon as I can work out some schedule issues, I'll contact you about an initial visit. It sounds like fun.

To: Eurogang Steering Committee – Esbensen, Maxson, Medina, van Gemert, Weerman

I wanted to let you know of yet another development in our Eurogang enterprise. I have just accepted an invitation from Prof. Martin Keller, Criminology Institute, Free University of Euroburg, to serve as consultant to his new project. He has been funded by local officials to undertake a research project in his city where street gangs have suddenly become a cause célèbre. I'll be visiting Martin and his research team soon, and probably occasionally thereafter. I'm letting you know because it is his intention to employ our research instruments in the project and will be asking your approval to do so (or, perhaps he has done this already). I like this opportunity to observe someone else, at close hand, using (and not abusing) our instruments. It also occurred to me that our forthcoming EG IX workshop might take advantage of what he's doing in Euroburg. Perhaps one of more of our workshop students could end up working comparatively with Martin's students.

It never ceases to amaze me that the Eurogang Program, always at the edges of poverty and opportunity, keeps finding new ways to renew itself. Here we are, ten years later, and just like the Energizer Bunny we keep going and going!

10. Euroburg Visited

To: Cheryl Maxson cmaxson@uci.edu

A little while ago, you got my memo to you and the others on the Eurogang Steering Committee. This is a follow-up just to you, because you are so familiar with my travel reports. Well, I'm in Euroburg – just for a few days to get a sense of the place. I squeezed it in between a couple of other site visits but mostly because I came over for the September meetings of the European Society of Criminology in Bologna. I'll come back next month to put in some genuine consulting time.

I haven't hooked up with Martin Keller's team on this visit, but Martin and his quite charming wife have given me a walking tour of parts of the city (incidentally, she's as outgoing and informal as he is quiet and, in truth, a bit stiff). My camera has been working overtime, especially to accommodate to the weather. There's been a low pressure system over the whole area for some days. This results in higher than normal humidity with mists emanating from the river in the distance and the canal that bisects the city. When I try for pictures up on the castle hill, I capture only turrets and church steeples poking up from the gray layer below. And when I'm down in the streets, the turrets and steeples don't exist. I'm told this is not uncommon here in the fall months.

You would find familiar things here in Euroburg. Its population is similar to a number of our collaboration cities – Copenhagen, Bremen, Manchester, the Hague, Oslo, Frankfurt, Toulouse, Stockholm for instance – but not including broader metropolitan areas. Euroburg quickly disappears beyond its immediate suburbs into fields and low hills with orchards and vineyards along the river. It is definitely not of the size or complexity of our larger sites, like London, Amsterdam, Berlin, Barcelona, Paris, and the like. We're in the 500,000 to 700,000 population range here.

Major industries include tourism, shipping, commercial trading, and light manufacturing, but no heavy industry. And while there is overall heterogeneity if you consider the city as a whole, it actually breaks down into a number of distinct districts. There is an older area of considerable wealth associated with commercial success over the centuries. There's a working class area that has seen better days – far better. The Old Town area, as you might expect, is the tourist mecca with many boutiques, craft stores, a variety of restaurants, and small old hotels. Along the canal there are scores of wharfs where the shipping business is concentrated, and also a lot of houseboats more of less permanently stationed to form a narrow, watery suburb. Beyond the canal is much of the new post-war town with track housing, apartments, and condos, and beyond that are a large, light industry complex and the immigrant housing areas known unhappily as "The Middle East." The last of these is the source of the major gang problems that led to the Keller project. Euroburg is about 20 percent "foreign."

Judging from my tour, the more "integrated" immigrant workers run the taxis and buses, work in the subways, handle street work and janitorial services, and food services (look in the kitchens of Italian, German, French, and "continental" restaurants and you'll find the cooks are middle-eastern, Moroccan, Pakistani, and so on, but the food is not). Muslim women clean the rooms and halls of my hotel; my bartender identifies himself as Greek (I asked because he keeps Ouzo prominently displayed. In his honor, of course, I drink it – carefully). Frankly, I don't see a lot of native Euroburgers in the low-pay and part-time occupations. The old guest worker programs of the 1950s and 1960s and beyond seem to have become a permanent economic (and housing and employment) feature of life here. Martin tells me the main subway traffic in the mornings is from the Middle East to Old Town, with the reverse in the late evenings. I'll hit some highlights for you, half based on what I've seen and half based on what the Kellers have told me.

Main shopping area in town: this is partially a cobblestone pedestrian mall closed off to all vehicular traffic except for the small trucks that supply the stores and restaurants. The regulars are here – mid- and upper range clothing stores, specialty shops, all the brands found in all central shopping areas. McDonalds and Burger King are here, of course. On the side streets, smaller businesses and tradesmen hang out their trade and guild symbols. The few homeless people I've seen stay in these side streets, but venture for money to the intersections with the cobblestone mall. At other corners one passes the street musicians varying from Bach to rock – guitars, drums, violins, accordions, even a bassoon duet. The Hare Krishna chanters are here as well. Not the mall streets, but the narrow side streets feature some very tight, often creative parking solutions. Some of these "solutions" are also the source of lewd confrontations which draw amused bystanders to see yet another street performance.

The mall is anchored on one end by the old town hall and cathedral, both of which front on the town square. On the other, it climbs gently into Old Town, a warren of narrow, winding streets, some again closed to most traffic. Keller's wife came into her own in this section of her town because of her familiarity with the gift, craft, and art stores. All these streets are cobblestone, in some of which you can still see the ruts made by horse-driven wagons and carriages of past centuries. The buildings range from 14th (!) to 17th century in origin. The basic structures are indeed that old, and all reconstructions are made to strict code to retain the original form and designs. Mrs. Keller lays this on both civic pride and the centrality of tourism to the economy – no tourists, no need for Old Town. Many of the buildings are stucco or stone with half-timbered accents, piled one on another with separation enough for one-way carriage traffic. Some of the old basements now serve as cellar restaurants and bars. Other cafés include both inside and outside seating, especially those around the small central plaza at the top of the hill from which the more popular streets drop down like spokes of a bicycle wheel. We had lunch (spaghetti and fish, with local white wine) in the smallest of these cafés and watched the odd admixture of tourists, local shop-owners, and a few gypsies plying their trade in front of a small Romanesque church which seemed to have no parishioners (but a lovely carillon ringing out at noon). What the Kellers didn't see, but I did, was several swastika graffitis on the walls, with the tag OTS above them. Are there skinheads in Euroburg? Keller doesn't know.

Next we went down to the canal and by the docks that used to bring visitors to Old Town. Now they have fish stalls and moorings for small boats. Across a long pedestrian bridge over the canal brings one to the base of low limestone cliffs above which are some terraced gardens leading up to the ruins of the count's castle. We turned left (I'll catch the castle on another day) along a row of very substantial piers where the canal comes alive with commercial traffic: small ships, industrial and coal barges, and this day two river cruise ships. Just north of this shore is a large area of mixed new and old residential sections. The apartments and condos farther out are of little interest, but the old residences – again, by old I mean 17th and 18th century – are the solid homes of the solid merchants and guilds that established Euroburg when the canal was originally cut to turn a sleepy town into a hub of commerce.

As you walk down the streets, you pass large double doors on massive iron hinges. When open, as they usually are, you face high entry ways designed for horse-drawn carriages to enter large courtyards towered over by multi-storied homes of those early inhabitants; merchants, politicians, court personnel and clerics (but not the bishop). Some of the courtyards retain their old charm, some are barren and untended, and some are now subdivided into apartments for middle and working class families. Few of Euroburg's immigrants, Keller points out, can afford such digs, nor even the newer apartment buildings beyond this section of town.

The Kellers make sure I point my camera upward, toward the iron grill balconies, the old guild and artisan signs, the well-tended flower pots in many windows, and the laundry – from underwear to bedsheets – hanging over balconies and along ropes between them. The electric dryer has not come to many homes.

What they don't point out, but is obvious to me, is that the post-war reconstruction in Old Town did not get to many of these older residential buildings. Occasionally, public buildings and churches have pictures of wartime destruction and restoration projects. The message is unclear: War is hell? We are survivors? Euroburg lives forever? Some of the old buildings still reveal bullet holes and shrapnel wounds. Old materials are of necessity replaced by newly invented quick fixes. Post-war quaint is often not so quaint. After bombing and artillery barrages, reconstruction can follow the form but not the true substance of what used to be. Curving streets of glass and brick are not the same as old stone and oak timbering. New statuary does not adequately replace the old. Euroburg, like much of Europe generally, adds the ruins of new wars to the original Roman ruins still visible and preserved under glass. It would be better not to play war.

Just as we were about to head west to conclude our tour, we were interrupted by a god-awful noise, or so it seemed at first. We had come upon the annual concert of the bells, a very special event for the guild of bell ringers. Each church in Euroburg, in a kind of challenge, rings out its own pattern. We actually see men pulling the ropes to swing the bells; at one small Romanesque church, the ringer stands on the sidewalk with a rope dangling from an opening in the bell tower. Although the carillon attached to St. Agnes Cathedral in the town square dominates the contest, most of the ringing bells are not cathedral-style chimes but more like enormous cow bells, giving off a fascinating cacophony of clangs and pings and gongs. It's the answering rhythm from tower to tower that makes it work. You find yourself drawn to the syncopation, straining to find some music to it all.

Our final piece of the tour – gratefully final, given my jet lag – is to an area known as the Backwater Canals. Created almost inadvertently with the canal's early expansion to handle larger river traffic, this is a low lying area at the western turn of the canal. It was flooded unintentionally, and then dredged out to narrow, winding mini-canals, barely wide enough to allow two boats to row past each other. Around these little canals grew up a distinct district of "affordable" housing – cheap, small, densely packed, subject to flooding every spring. Remember the wonderfully quaint canals of Bruges in Belgium? Well, this is Bruges gone to pot. It's called backwater canals for good reason. No tourists wandering around here.

We visited this so Keller could be fair and show me the worst of Euroburg (the worst, that is, unless one thinks of the suburban "Middle East" housing developments as part of the city). In our American terms, the Backwater Canals are Euroburg's slums, inhabited not by any of the immigrant populations but by the perennially unsuccessful local families – generations of them according to Keller. Again, he didn't seem to notice, but there are wall graffiti here of swastikas and OTS. If these tags match those in Old Town (and I believe they do – same form, same paint) then Keller's team is going to be doing some Skinhead research, with a chance to compare Euroburg to Oslo, Copenhagen, Stockholm, much of Germany and some of England.

That's it for now. It's a city worthy of some time spent, and seemingly a good addition to our Eurogang enterprise. I'll keep you and our Steering Committee apprised of developments.

11. The Zealots

Patrick van der Waal grew up in the small Dutch town of Nunspeet. Aside from occasional visits to Groningen and Amsterdam, he had little experience with urban life. The opportunity to study for a degree in communications and journalism at the Free University of Euroburg seemed irresistible – a new area, a new life in "the big city." Upon graduation, young van der Waal served as an intern at the Euroburg Daily News, and within three years had become that paper's lead crime reporter. It sounded exciting, but turned out to be fairly pedestrian as most crime was minor – domestic disputes, muggings of tourists, drunken escapades on the subway, hints of corruption in the city council. Most stories started in the police station, relied on police statistics, and ended with police announcements of police arrests and case clearances.

Van der Waal wanted more; he knew a good headline was valuable, a newsworthy story was the goal, and connecting the dots was how a good story was made. Street gangs in Euroburg provided the dots; he would seek out the connections. He decided on two approaches. One was to reconnect with Alexander Aziz, the Pakistani street worker he had quoted in his June 19 news story. Aziz could be Patrick's entry into the Zealots with whom he worked. The second was to do background research on "The Village" and its residents, the home base of the Zealots. It was Patrick's additional thought that, with the dots connected, he might get close to Professor Keller's operation and team as a further source of news materials. Patrick knew that being an "informant" for high profile news stories appealed to many people. He was perfectly willing to work Aziz, the professor, and others to make the Euroburg gang story his story.

Patrick already knew that Fort Araby, home to the Smokes, was hard to penetrate, whereas the Village was far more open. He possessed city records (reporters know the access points) and visited the Village over the summer months. Alexander, now his new "friend," was helpful in this research. Fort Araby was more Moroccan than Turkish, with the opposite the case in the Village. Alexander was a third generation Pakistani Euroburger who no longer lived in The Middle East but in an apartment nearer the canal with his mother and two younger brothers. His Pakistani father remained in the Village; his Russian mother – thus the name Alexander – had wanted "Sasha" as she called him and his brothers to get out of the Middle East and its troubles. Alexander was therefore an outside insider, trying to help his compatriots integrate into Euroburg life. Moroccan or Turk mattered little to him; the area also had smatterings of poorly assimilated second generation Kosovars, Greeks, Pakistanis, Lebanese, and most recently legal and illegal Afghan and Iraqi refugees. For Alexander, all marginalized youth shared a common outsider status and needed inroads to better housing, schooling, and job opportunities. He worked to provide these as a street worker for the state ministry of immigration.

Patrick had the statistics. Alexander showed him how they played out in the Village. Mostly two-story apartment-style housing accommodated large families. Typical would be a grandmother, father and mother – and sometimes the father's second wife – half a dozen siblings as well, often with one or more aunts, uncles, and cousins. The place was crowded, but nowhere as destitute as Fort Araby.

Outside were two mosques, religious schools, makeshift soccer fields, and the Village's major asset, the open air market of sheltered and open stalls. Here, residents of Fort Araby and the Village mingled actively with indigenous Euroburgers around the stalls; pistachios, glazed almonds and other nuts in this one; spices like chili, saffron, paprika, curry, ginger, garlic in that one; teas, dried herbs, roots, dried peppers, green raisins in another; thin-skinned citrus, dried apricots and other fruits in yet another. There are vendors for cooked meats – chicken, duck, lamb – and clothing materials like sheepskin for shoes, plain dark cottons for burkas, colorful cottons for everything hidden beneath the burkas, lace for face veils, and so on. It's a bazaar, and a place to meet, to observe, and – for the young – to frolic and pick pockets. The police do not appear here. Some of the Zealots (but no rival Smokes) can be found here, and on his visits Patrick is introduced to them by Alexander, or "Pasha Sasha," the street name they have given him.

Alexander also has Patrick meet his two younger fellow workers, Muzafer and Abu, a "Paki" and an Afghan, both refugees from war-torn border areas between their home countries. Both have seen hell, and want to turn their experiences into something positive for their younger peers. They explain to Patrick (who will surely use their comments in his writing) that the Zealots/Smokes rivalry is nothing compared to the tribal wars they have seen, so their entrée into the world of the Zealots was easy, and they understand as well the family breakdown, school failures, and limited job skills and opportunities that left the Zealots on the streets, depending on each other and finding cohesiveness in their gang. "There's nothing hidden about all this," said Abu, "so why are the police and the welfare people so ignorant about it?"

Muzafer described the only time he saw direct police intervention in the occasional gang rivalry between Fort Araby and the Village. At a wedding party in a second floor apartment used by the Smokes, a militant Turkish youth from the Village attempted to "assassinate" a Smokes elder. To escape the vengeful Moroccans, he leapt out a window to the concrete walkway below, breaking his leg. When wedding guests ran down and found him there, they began to beat him mercilessly. "Miraculously," as Muzafer described it, a young rookie Euroburg policeman happened on the scene and attempted to intervene. He, too, was mercilessly beaten. "Maybe that's why we never see the coppers here in the Middle East," added Abu. Patrick van der Waal had his next Euroburg gang story.

His next ploy, connecting the dots further, was to set up a meeting between the three Zealot workers and Professor Keller's team, with himself as the liaison. But he succeeded only partially. A series of phone calls and e-mails led to the meeting, but with Keller agreeing with Heinrich that the press had no place in their research. The task of inviting the workers and dis-inviting reporter van der Waal fell to Magda, who managed both parts with professional tact; Patrick agreed to wait for a first shot at "the big story" in Magda's terms, while Alexander, Muzafer, and Abu appeared at the institute to share their knowledge and give their Zealots the "legitimacy" of university attention.

As she described it later to the consultant, Magda viewed the meeting not only as a success, but as a pivotal event in the project, adding that Prof. Keller had carried off a masterful joining of forces. By the end, she said, the team had expanded to include three street workers, albeit as volunteers rather than employees. They and Keller's four students found their national and cultural differences to fade in favor of their mutual concerns for the socially excluded youth of Euroburg. Keller had Heinrich start things off by describing what he and Liz had learned about the Smokes of Fort Araby. There was much head-nodding by Alexander, Muzafer, and Abu as Heinrich spelled out the data – his term – from the agency people, the elders at the Akbar Café, and his gang informants.

The Zealot workers were particularly intrigued by the internal structure of the Smokes. Because their history had gone back several decades, not long after Fort Araby had become a distinct ethnic community, the Smokes had developed a series of age-graded subgroups or cliques. The oldest, called elders by some and "O.G.'s" by others (original gangsters, borrowed from American gang argot), had all but given up the gang life, many in fact having returned to their home countries several times. Below them were at least three other age cliques: the original "Duskies" now in their twenties, the Central Smokes of later adolescence, and the Young Smokes more recently joined around ages 13 to 15. Heinrich also described even younger hangers – on who seemed destined to carry on the Smokes tradition but had not yet coalesced into a self-defined clique. They were, Heinrich noted, mere babies at ages nine, ten, and eleven.

Alexander and his two workers countered with a different description of most Zealots. They were first generation youth, as often refugee as immigrant, and the group had a history of less than ten years. Mostly school-based adolescents, they had not formed the cliques described by Heinrich, and were considerably more politically or nationally oriented than the Smokes. Sharia law was often mentioned in the Village. In response to queries from Liz, both Muzafer and Abu argued not only that there were no female Zealot members, but that the idea seemed almost ludicrous. Gang-banging was men's work, and there was more than enough work at home to occupy the girls. They had tasks to perform for their families, and certainly should not be seen in public in the company of boys. Heinrich and Liz understood this pattern, but saw cracks in the gender fabric among the Smokes.

As she continued to describe the meeting at the Institute, Magda took pride in the openness of both groups, but particularly in Keller's handling of the critical issue: Why should Alexander and his workers continue to work with the researchers? They walked right into Keller's web when he asked them what *they* wanted from a continuing dialogue. Alexander's answer was reflexive and instantaneous – money for his Zealots, who were closed off from jobs and surrounded by family poverty.

A deal was struck. Keller described briefly his need for gang ethnographies, entailing having Dirk and Conrad able to hang around the Village with the support and legitimacy that the workers could provide. In addition, Dirk and Conrad would carry out in-depth interviews with selected and willing Zealots, for which the respondents would be well paid for their time and also for setting up further interviews with other Village youth in "snowball" fashion. Data for the project, money for the boys, and as Abu suggested, more respect for the Village youth than they had ever received from outsiders.

Other details would be worked out. Cell phone numbers were exchanged, the ultimate symbol of intentional collaboration. Magda would see to the arrangements and the specifics of the needed "data" would be described. Heinrich for the Smokes and Alexander for the Zealots would be in contact should difficulties arise between the groups as they became more obvious targets of attention. For now, it was noted, Smoke/Zealot conflict was minimal as each gang was territorially distinct and had few "beefs." Finally, it was agreed that any public inquiries would be referred to the professor. In particular, reporter van der Waal was not to be engaged except by Keller; this collaboration was a project, not a story. And it was now a two-gang comparative research project, sensitive both to local needs and to the knowledge-building enterprise. Professor Keller remained in the conference room after the others had departed, a small, satisfied smile on his face and puffing away at his empty pipe.

12. Background Statement: The Street Gang Typology

As the Euroburg research team was learning, no two street gangs are exactly alike. They differ in the nature of the neighborhoods they inhabit, in their ethnicity, size, and duration, in the characteristics of their members, in their behavior and crime patterns, and in the group processes that maintain them over time as well as at any point in time. In addition, the character of each gang may change over time. Yet if we allow these sources of variation to dominate our views of street gangs, then we will end up with only anecdotal and case study pictures of gangs, not a "science" of gangs.

This outcome is not acceptable. We must be able to see beyond the particular to the general, beyond single descriptions to patterns of street gang existence. This is the importance of a consensus definition of street gangs, such as that offered by the Eurogang Program: *A street gang is any durable, street-oriented youth group whose involvement in illegal activity is part of its group identity.*

Beyond a common, measurable definition, we must strive for reliable *patterns* of gangs, a gang typology, that brings some order to the often dramatic and intriguing nature of individual gangs. Members of the Eurogang Program based in the U.S. have developed such a typology, a specifically *structural* typology, and applied it with considerable success across hundreds of gangs in the U.S. and scores of gangs throughout Europe. It is known as the Maxson/Klein street gang typology (see Chapter 5 in their *Street Gang Patterns and Policies*) and should be applicable to a setting like Euroburg.

The typology emerged from an inductive analysis of the structural properties of the gangs best known to police gang specialists in 60 cities. It was then tested and modified in a survey in over 200 cities. The result, a five-fold typology, was then independently validated in every gang-involved town and city in the state of Illinois by a state research organization, and again nationally by the federally funded National Youth Gang Center. Finally, it was tested again in the original 60 cities to assess the typology results over time. This process was far, far more extensive than any previous attempt. It "worked," in the important sense that the five types encompassed between 75 percent and 90 percent of all street gangs (depending on the particular validating study). The five street gang types are represented in the following scenarios.

The Traditional Gang Traditional gangs have generally been in existence for 20 or more years: they keep regenerating themselves. They contain fairly clear subgroups, usually separated by age. O.G.'s ("Original Gangsters") or Veteranos, Seniors, Juniors, Midgets, and various other names are applied to these different age-based cliques. Sometimes, the cliques are separated by neighborhood rather than age. More than other gangs, traditional gangs tend to have a wide range of their members, sometimes as wide as from 9 to 10 years of age into the 30s. These are usually very large gangs, numbering a hundred or even several hundred members. Almost always, they are territorial in the sense that they identify strongly with their turf, 'hood, or barrio and claim it as theirs alone.

In sum, this is a large, enduring, territorial gang with a wide age range and several internal cliques based on age or area.

The Neotraditional Gang The neotraditional gang resembles the traditional form, but has not been in existence as long – probably no more than 10 years and often less. It may be of medium size – say 50 to 100 members – or number its members in the hundreds. It probably has developed subgroups or cliques based on age or area, but sometimes may not. Like traditional gangs, it is also very territorial, claiming turf and defending it.

In sum, the neotraditional gang is a newer territorial gang that looks to be on its way to becoming traditional in time. Thus, at this point it is subgrouping, but may or may not have achieved territoriality, and its size suggests that it is evolving into the traditional form.

The Compressed Gang The compressed gang is small – usually in the size range of up to 50 members – and has not formed subgroups. The age range is probably narrow – 10 or fewer years between the younger and older members. The small size, absence of subgroups, and narrow age range may reflect the newness of the group, in existence less than 10 years and maybe for only a few years. Some of these compressed gangs have become territorial, but many have not.

In sum, compressed gangs have a relatively short history, short enough that by size, duration, subgrouping, and territoriality, it is unclear whether they will grow and solidify into the more-traditional forms or simply remain as less-complex groups.

The Collective Gang The collective gang looks like the compressed form, but bigger and with a wider age range – maybe 10 or more years between younger and older members. Size can be under 100 but is probably larger. Surprisingly, given these numbers, it has not developed subgroups and may or may not be a territorial gang. It probably has a 10- to 15-year existence.

In sum, the collective gang resembles a kind of shapeless mass of adolescent and young adult members and has not developed the distinguishing characteristics of other gangs.

The Specialty Gang Unlike the other gangs, which engage in a wide variety of criminal offenses, crime in this type of group is narrowly focused on a few offenses; the group comes to be characterized by the specialty. The specialty gang tends to be small – usually 50 or fewer members – without any subgroups in most cases (there are exceptions). It probably has a history of less than 10 years but has developed a well-defined territory. Its territory may be either residential or based on the opportunities for the particular form of crime in which it specializes. The age range of most specialty gangs is narrow, but in a few others broad.

In sum, the specialty gang is crime-focused in a narrow way. Its principal purpose is more criminal than social, and its smaller size and form of territoriality may be a reflection of this focused crime pattern.

In applying a made-in-the-USA model to Europe, questions inevitably arise. Four have emerged as paramount: its stability over time, its transferability to Europe, the specific labels of the five types, and acceptable approaches to measuring any gang as fitting into one of the types.

As to stability, the original researchers found some variation across the five types over a four-year period. Traditional and compressed gangs most commonly remained true to form. Collective gangs were most likely to develop into one of the other forms. Specialty gangs were more likely to dissolve, but overall stability or alteration of form was far more common than outright dissolution. Studies of gang types must be concerned with both form and transformation.

The transferability of the typology to the European theater, skeptically received at first by some Eurogang researchers, has proven to be a relatively minor problem. An increasing number of European case studies of gangs have explicitly assessed sub-grouping, size, age, duration, territoriality, and crime versatility. In most cases, doing so has allowed the researchers to fit their gangs into the five slots. In several cases, e.g. Manchester, Stockholm, and the Netherlands, several gangs in each location could be placed under separate categories. In at least two instances, Oslo, Norway and Kazan, Russia, special circumstances made the typology less applicable. Interestingly, in both cases there has been a transformation of street gangs into adult, criminal cartels. But with such exceptions noted, it is increasingly clear that the U.S.-born typology fits with the nature of the emerging gang scene in Europe. The "empirical question" has received an empirical answer.

A minor but interesting third issue has been raised, that of the labels applied to the five types. The terms traditional and therefore neo-traditional, satisfying in the U.S., are less so in Europe. This is because in Europe the word "traditional" is more commonly used to describe the customs, costumes, and conservative attitudes of the various nations. It has been agreed among the Eurogang researchers that one can employ the alternative terminology of Classical and Neo-Classical street gangs with no loss in meaning.

The final issue has to do with how to assess a gang's type when using either surveys or ethnographies. Two approaches are available, although only the first is required in the Eurogang measuring instruments while the second is an available option. In the first, the interview schedule or the ethnographic guidelines include assessments of the respondents' gang status as to the defining structural dimensions. That is, one measures sub-grouping, size, ages, duration, territoriality, and crime versatility. It is then up to the researcher to use these data to recreate the gang type according to the five descriptions or scenarios.

The second measurement approach, more direct but perhaps more difficult to handle, is to present the five scenarios to the respondent (adult or youth) who has an admitted group or gang affiliation. The respondent reviews the five and selects the one which best fits his group. If any one of the five fits, then his group *is* by definition a street gang of that type.

Whichever choice is made, there is the clear opportunity to overcome single-case mentality and seek *patterns* of gang form across cities and across countries. In Euroburg, there is already evidence, with more to come, that the Smokes and the Zealots are of different types, most likely traditional and compressed to judge from reports by Heinrich and by Alexander and his co-workers. This will help to place Euroburg street gangs in the context of such gangs in many other European settings. Comparative analyses should emerge.

13. Gang Workers at Risk

The late October staff meeting was scheduled for 9:00 a.m. The team members were punctual – Magda had set the norm for that at earlier meetings – but the invited Zealot team had not yet appeared. They had been specially invited because of the day's topic: preparations for the extended visit of the American consultant who was flying in that evening. Keller had two things in mind. The first was getting the students as well as Magda and himself prepared to report their experiences to date, and getting Alexander's worker team into the spirit of the project as a research adventure that went beyond mere advocacy for socially excluded youth.

The second agenda item was discussing what everyone hoped to get from the consultant. In truth, this really meant what Keller wanted them to get, but he phrased it as a group process. He had in mind such things as learning more about the Eurogang research instruments and how they could yield comparable data; issues of sampling experts, youth, and field observations; descriptions of street gangs already studied in the Eurogang Program; and handling public relations issues with community leaders, residents of gang neighborhoods, and the press (Patrick van der Waal remained a lurking presence).

With the Zealot workers still missing, Keller started the discussion in reverse order – how could they foster healthy but not risky relationships with the gang neighborhoods. He could not know how prescient he was: at 9:30 Alexander came through the conference room door, all but carrying Abu at his side. And what a mess Abu was, bringing gasps and "Oh my Gods" from the staff. As he was lowered into a chair at the table, Magda moved to his side to coo over him.

His face looked like a painted potato: puffed eyes, swollen cheeks, blue bruises and red cuts and scratches, one ear covered in a large bandage and the other beet red. When he tried to smile at Magda, it revealed several missing front teeth. Heinrich tried to see the smile again; "Seen any good boxing matches lately," he asked but drew no laughter, and a deep scowl from Keller. Abu could mumble, but not speak clearly at all. It was Alexander who provided the story.

Abu and Muzafer had been with some of the Zealots late the previous night at the railway station, running through the tunnel to catch the subway back to the Middle East. It had been a fruitless Sunday night – no action, no Euroburger girls to hassle, no tourists careless with their camera bags. At the end of the tunnel they came upon a large collection of Smokes, including some of the elders. With a confrontation obviously possible, Muzafer and Abu intervened between the groups quickly, and seemingly effectively. The Zealots held back after a lot of threatening verbal challenges had been exchanged, while the Smokes moved forward to enter the front cars of the arriving subway.

Then Abu made a mistake. Instead of staying back with his boys, he ran after some of the elder Smokes to reinforce his peace-making initiative. He was pulled into the front car and the subway left the station. At the next stop, near the Akbar Café, the Smokes exited the train, dumping Abu on the platform where he was assisted by other passengers and then taken to the city hospital's emergency treatment ward.

Thanks to cell phones Muzafer was soon at the hospital, followed by Alexander and later by Sgt. Mellers when the hospital reported the assault. Little could please Andre Mellers more than investigating a gang assault against a social worker, for whom he would have less than full respect in any case, victim or not.

After a series of x-rays and MRI's revealed no broken bones and no apparent internal injuries, Abu was patched up and put to bed to determine whether a concussion had any lasting effect. In the early morning, he was released with treatment instructions to Alexander, while Muzafer was detained further by Sgt. Mellers as a witness to be interviewed. Abu insisted on being taken to the project staff meeting, and thus his dramatic entrance just as the group was talking about neighborhood relationships.

Obviously, Keller's agenda was abandoned. Abu was the new agenda, and then this too changed when Muzafer arrived. Sgt. Mellers, he reported, thought maybe the beating was intended to send a message from the Smokes elders, and Muzafer agreed. "For God's sake, a message to whom?" shrieked Liz. Muzafer and Alexander looked at her solicitously, and then in tandem they pointed at Heinrich. "Oh my God" spilled out of Liz as she rose to put her arms around Heinrich – not Abu, but Heinrich. Muzafer explained:

"I've seen this before, back home. There was no attempt to kill, or permanently damage. The purpose is to make the effect as visible as possible, like waving a large flag. I think they were saying to Heinrich, 'You're getting too close, you're intruding in *our* world. Back off.' And I think he should; he has said he was warned about this before by a guy named Samurai. They don't call him Heinrich the Hound without reason."

The ensuing discussion got more complex and more intense. Abu could only listen, and mumble, and groan now and then. Magda stayed by his side, magically producing aspirin as needed. Keller now led the discussion, knowing full well where he wanted it to end up but seeming to give equal credence to each of three alternatives: pull out, pull back, or go in only as teams of two.

Pulling out was unacceptable to everyone. First, they were hired by the city to do a job. One incident couldn't justify quitting. Second, pride emerged vigorously. Abu was down, but determined to rise up again. Alexander and Muzafer felt sure the assault was not targeted at them; in fact, they could use it to their advantage, to return to their boys with new respect. And Heinrich was not about to quit, or show fear, or even acknowledge the validity of a threat to him if indeed that's what it was. Only Liz was hesitant. This was *her* Heinrich, after all. So she made the suggestion that Keller had been planning to make. One of the other students, or else someone hired from Fort Araby or the broader Moroccan community, would team up with Heinrich for a while. This would increase safety, "diffuse the blame" as Keller put it, and incidentally speed up the research process in Fort Araby.

Dirk broke in: "I've lived around Moroccans in Amsterdam most of my life. I know them, I know the culture, I've had Moroccan Rif friends. I could be a legitimate street researcher in Fort Araby. If you teach me ethnography, Professor, it will solve the problem and give me really good experience. Let me go in with Hein."

And there it was. The danger was acknowledged and a seemingly suitable adjustment was made. But lest things look too easy, Alexander threw in a special warning. "Muzafer and Abu know this, but the rest of you don't. Two years ago, after I was hired by the immigration ministry to go into the Middle East, I was driving my little Fiat from Castle Hill toward the Middle East. At a stop sign, another car pulled up next to me and the front passenger pointed a hand gun at my head through the window. Then the driver and passenger laughed and pulled ahead of me. I didn't know them, but they drove on toward Fort Araby. I'll admit I was scared, although I think they were just showing their balls – didn't know yet who I was or what I was. But Heinrich, don't get ballsy yourself. Show these guys you really respect them, or that gun could go off." "Amen," said Liz, as the meeting broke up.

Keller again remained after them all, puffing that empty pipe but without the smile. Magda came in and sat with him, quietly. They would meet the American consultant that evening, with an additional agenda item.

14. Background Statement: Group Processes; What Makes a Gang a Gang?

[Special Comments from the Author]

How does it get to this, that violence becomes a means of communication? Already we have had the gun at Alexander's head, the comment of Muhammad H. to Heinrich about the use of his fists, and the message purportedly sent in the assault on Abu. The answer lies in the special group processes that are to be found in street gangs.

Gang are not merely collections of individuals; the gang as a group takes on additional properties (think about five individuals shooting baskets against five other individuals, versus a *team* of five combining and melding their skills as group unit against another team of five). Groups have unique properties – cohesiveness, structure, leadership, group histories and standards, common goals, and internal frictions. Good team coaches recognize these and use them to improve performance. Those intervening with gangs also would benefit from such knowledge to reduce "team" performance among gangs.

But law enforcement and prevention and intervention agencies must recognize as well that street gangs have special attributes beyond those found in most other groups. These attributes are the critical factors that make gangs qualitatively different from other youth groups, factors that on their own have been shown to defeat our efforts at gang control. Four of these were discussed in Chapter 4.

1. Street gang members are drawn principally from marginalized populations. Thus they start off feeling different, subject to prejudice and discriminatory practices, and somewhat alienated, left out of the mainstream. Resentment, fatalism, and lack of hope give them common bonds; groups need common bonds.

2. Street gangs develop an "oppositional culture", an us-against-them mentality that leads them to reject efforts to serve and help them, and increases their antagonism toward those who wish to control them. Everything we do to them and for them gets reinterpreted as being against them. Our messages delivered are transformed into different messages received by them. The greatest builder of gang cohesiveness may be rival gangs, but the next is probably outsiders – adult authorities – who intervene in the gang's life.

3. Crime involvement – the identity in illegal activity of our definition – provides a "tipping point" that separates the street gang from what it was before. This places criminal activity in a positive light, as a common bond to increase the us-against-them mentality.

4. Violence, in particular, acts as a unifier in the street gang world. It's not so much the acts of violence that's important; many gangs are low in violence and many members commit few violent acts. But the rhetoric of violence is important in binding members to each other. "War stories", retelling of real and mythical exploits, play-fighting and threats, perceived threats from outside, become a minor mantra within the gang, an extra unifier on top of everything else.

5. Cohesiveness, the bonds that tie group members to each other, is central to individual gang membership and to maintaining group strength. Most gangs are not very cohesive, but can be made more so by our efforts to intervene with them. Cliques are usually more cohesive than overall gang structures – it's hard to have a truly cohesive group of 50 or 100 more members – but the potential for increased cohesiveness is always there, and increased gang cohesiveness leads to

increased gang crime and violence. We must avoid the unintended increase in cohesiveness that may result from our efforts at control.

6. Crime amplification is a common result of gang membership, as shown in many long-term studies of street gangs. New recruits tend to be somewhat more involved in illegal activity than those who do not join gangs. But the major pattern takes place after joining. The effect of group processes on new members is to increase their criminal involvement dramatically – a group effect. And when members reduce and then cease their gang membership, as almost all do eventually, their criminal activity decreases just as dramatically. As the group processes weaken, the resultant crime decreases as well. Normal desistance from gang membership may be our best hope.

7. The relationship between gang cohesiveness and gang violence is often pivotal. Even though most violence is verbal, rhetorical, and minor, the concern with violence feeds the special group feeling we call cohesiveness. Reciprocally, the more cohesive cliques, if not gangs as a whole, are more likely to engage in violence, especially symbolic (message-sending) and retaliatory violence. In the gang, as in almost no other youth group, violent behavior is not only tolerated or acceptable, it is glorified and legitimated. When cohesiveness dwindles, it is often words or acts of violence that are called upon to bring group cohesiveness back up.

8. Of many common misconceptions about street gangs, one of the most common is that gangs are formed (occasionally they are) and directed (again, occasionally they are) by strong individual leaders. This is seldom the case, especially in the larger traditional and Neo-traditional types. Rather, leadership is diffused over cliques and across different activities (partying, sports, drug dealing, intergang violence and so on). Rather than strong leadership, it is the striving for status and respect that more often drives individual behavior in the gang. Police and social workers who hope to reduce gang activity by arresting or reforming those they define as gang "leaders" will be continually frustrated. Leadership tends to be functional, ephemeral, and replaceable, not stable. Gang leadership is more a romantic myth than an operational fact.

Finally, research has shown that group process in street gangs trumps ethnicity and nationality, as well as neighborhood. These latter variables are salient, yes, but they are more descriptors of gang contexts than definers of what separates street gangs from other youth groups. Those who would intervene in gang life without taking account of its special group processes will stumble badly. It was a lesson Abu learned painfully. Other lessons would follow in Euroburg.

15. The Consultant Settles In

Dear Margy;

It's 22 October, as we say here. My jet lag is passing and I'm settling into Euroburg and my three-star-plus hotel that Keller's funding is taking care of. Very nice, high up in Old Town, with a view down toward the canal that seems surprisingly busy with commercial traffic. I'll mail this letter at the hotel desk before going on to my first meeting at the Institute of Criminology with Martin's project staff. I know it will be interesting because of what I'll tell you next. Also, I'll try to list for you some of the Euroburg sights I've enjoyed over the past day and a half. It would be "déjà vu all over again" for you, as much of the city is like parts of the other gang cities we've visited since our sabbatical in Stockholm that started this whole thing off. You'd like it here – care to change your research schedule and join me?

I was met at the airport by Martin and driven straight to the hotel to freshen up before dinner. Actually, straight is not correct; Old Town as you would expect is all winding, narrow streets, with some closed off to vehicles. So we worked our way to the hotel. Two hours later, Magda, Martin's assistant – a real pistol, by the way – met me in the lobby and walked me to a charming cellar restaurant, much like those in Stockholm. On the way, we passed a homeless man, obviously disturbed, being berated by several youth who looked like skinheads to me. A policeman nearby watched the episode, but when the poor guy escaped into a deep excavation by the road, the skins moved on. The cop had done nothing to intervene. The excavation had a bronze plaque at its entrance: "Roman Temple Foundation, circa 600 A.D. Entry Prohibited." So, Margy, when will civilization really start?

Magda was triggered by the event to warn me. Three prior visiting professors over the past several years had not been sufficiently alert to their surroundings. One almost had his wallet and passport picked while in a crowd watching some street mimes perform. One had his camera bag stolen in a Burger King, of all places – Magda chuckled and pronounced it "Burglar King." The third had her airport carry-on "disappear" somewhere between entering an airport taxi and checking in at her hotel (not, she pointed out, my hotel). I assured Magda that after all these years I had learned to treat European streets as hostile territory.

Dinner held surprises not heralded by Magda, probably because she wouldn't want to up-stage Martin. He was there with Mrs. Keller, a really vivacious lady artist of some sort, and the deputy mayor. It turns out he's been fronting the project in the labyrinth of city hall. He is anxious to see that it is both protected and politically useful (whether to himself or the Mayor I couldn't make out). The restaurant fare was truly continental, so in your honor I ordered a mixed grill including slices of reindeer, steamed vegetables, crème brulè and let Martin choose a local dry red wine. Again in your honor, I had some white port afterwards.

But the food, good as it was, took second place to events two nights ago. Martin told the story, which neither his wife nor the deputy mayor had heard. It seems one of the street workers assigned to the Zealots, one of the project-identified gangs, went overboard in an attempt to intervene in a confrontation with the rival Smokes. He was badly beaten, taken to the ER, and showed up at the staff meeting Monday morning in pretty bad shape. His co-workers suggested that the assault (also reported to the police) was supposed to send a "back off" message to Martin's student, Heinrich, who has been aggressively seeking acceptance by the Smokes.

As a result, the staff has made some adjustments to their field operations, but Martin insists the event will not cause any disruption in the project. Magda seems less sure of this; she is closer to the students than is Martin. The deputy mayor immediately offered police protection for the staff, but I agreed with Martin and Magda that this would only close off data access. Still the deputy mayor is concerned for the project and asked me if such events were common. I assured him they were not (not sharing with him the Los Angeles events of which I've told you in the past). I'll speak with the group tomorrow about the event, however; I do find it worrisome. As you well know, I was once pinned between two fighting gang members, and also got word at one point that two brothers sought by the police had put out a "contract" on me. I was able to work my way out of it (else I might not be here to write this), but it surely left a lasting impression on me.

One other note about dinner is interesting. When we left the restaurant, a news reporter and photographer were waiting outside for us. Of course this has happened to me before when I didn't want coverage – in Philadelphia, in Oslo, in Madrid that I can recall off hand – but this time the deputy mayor earned his political credentials. He knew the reporter, who Martin said was trying hard to "infiltrate" the project, and moved him and his photographer down the street while the rest of us made a quick retreat. I doubt the deputy mayor will give them the worker assault story, since he understands it could make things tougher for "his" project. And indeed, the morning paper in the hotel lobby carried only a short story about an American gang expert coming into town to consult with city officials. The deputy mayor's name was prominently featured; Martin was only mentioned and my name was absent.

At this point I was ready for my hotel room, a cognac, and my bed. But the Kellers and Magda had other plans for me. We walked down to the town square and some temporary bleachers just beyond, at the edge of the canal. Fortuitously, this was the night of the annual water festival. We arrived in time to see the tail end of the parade of the boats (all decorated in colored lights) and then the highlight. This was the competing fireworks from various invited cities. One sits along the edge of the canal with baskets filled with beer, wine, cheese, and sausages amid hordes of other spectators to ooh and aah at the displays (Mrs. Keller had a cloth bag with two bottles of local red, some cheese and some crackers).

The show lasted well over an hour, with lavish fireworks displays set off in alphabetical order from this year's invitees from Barcelona, Frankfurt, Marseilles, Naples and Stockholm, with the finale provided by Euroburg. A large monetary prize and an automatic invitation for the next year goes to the winner as judged by a panel of past winners. Euroburg came in third, its best showing yet, but the Swedes were the winners (deservedly in my judgment) for the second year in a row. It is rumored that they hired a Chinese team to design their display which was, indeed, spectacular.

So, that was Monday, a long and eventful evening. I slept better than I usually do on these trips, so at 9:30 Magda met me to do her tour guide bit, showing me a few spots on *her* cultural list (and, I think, trying to gauge for herself just what I might offer the group). We started in a circuitous route through several Roman ruins locations – no homeless people this time – past but not into a small Roman Antiquities Museum built on the very site of the original Roman soldiers' encampment.

From there we crossed the canal on a pedestrian bridge to the area where many of the original guild halls had been built, and still serve as wealthy private residences and public buildings. Of most interest was a small, beautifully designed garden square with a series of statues, each representing one of the medieval guilds that had come together to plan the canal and thus (a) break the power of the bishop and (b) turn Euroburg into a thriving, middle class town.

So, what Magda was doing was *her* historical city. From Rome to the making of the city. Next I supposed I would see thriving, modern Euroburg, but no. The message turned out to be more like, "see our great cultural heritage, but see now how we have failed to live up to it." At least that's how I interpret her tour, because the next site, near the piers on the canal, was an ethnic restaurant row, with national variations on seafood (or canal and river food, I guess). Lots of dogs wandering about, including being allowed *in* the restaurants. Graffiti abounds here, mostly political but some individual tags and a few gang-style writings as well. One Arab café was particularly busy and Magda noted I'd be seeing more of these in the project areas. This one is loud with pop music, tea sets, and lots of men playing dominoes and backgammon. The other restaurants, in various stages of disrepair, in contrast with those I've seen in Old Town, were Chinese, Italian, German, Indian, and Pakistani, and odd mixtures of these and local cuisine.

The tour was over. To my great delight, Magda then took me into a Lutheran church to hear its daily noontime organ concert. There were only a dozen of us in there, and the music resonated around the simple white walls. It lasted only 30 minutes, unfortunately. We ended in a charming canal restaurant that was once a river barge. Good trout, a half-carafe of local white wine, and a wrap-up lecture from Magda. It went something like this:

"Poor Euroburg; it hasn't always been this way. The die was cast when the Romans retreated from their expansion and fortified their river defenses against the northern 'barbarians'. The Holy Roman Empire and the rising church states brought new forms of urban life and commerce. Locally, the expansion of the vineyards introduced from Rome and the rising strength of the guilds formed a new Euroburg, especially with the construction of the canal.

"Through all of this, and through all the wars and religious transformations, one thing remained contant: Euroburg was Caucasian, narrowly described. The expulsion of the Jews after the great plague was the only 'racial correction' ever entertained. Until, that is, there came the aftermath of the second world war with its decimation of the male working population and the industrial and agricultural explosion of the recovery period. Euroburg, like so many other cities, turned east and south to recruit immigrant labor, and then extended its welcome to refugee groups as well. They were to provide temporary forms of economic adjustment, but of course they never returned home."

By then, I'd had it, so I excused myself, returned across the canal to my hotel, and punched out. There's more of Euroburg I want to see, but jet lag trumps interest. I stayed in the hotel for dinner, watched CNN and Eurosports channels for a while, and crashed for the night. Tried to call you, but you were out gallivanting somewhere.

The next morning, Wednesday, I was fully recovered so I stuffed up on my very nice buffet breakfast, grabbed my city guide, and attacked what was left of touristy Euroburg. I'll do just a quick summary for you – pictures will tell the rest. First I wandered across the canal and turned west into 18th and 19th century areas. In succession, I came upon a glass-vaulted shopping arcade, full of specialty and chain stores under the vault that must have been at least three stories high. My favorite scene was of two adjacent stores: the first was the Gap with its uniform outfits of jeans, khakis and so on and the second was the *true* uniform store, where police and security guards can buy their full uniforms and accessories. Both store windows feature dressed dummies, but the police store mannequins are attractive pairs of male and female officers, all tall and blond with perfect posture.

Beyond this is the old armory with its shuttered windows in regional colors and emblems. Inside are various artisan shops – copper, silver, gold, china, antiques. This leads one to the architecturally grotesque army museum and the equally ugly army stables, old red and black brick structures with toy-castle turrets and balconies. It's ugly enough to be visually striking. And (understandably) next door is a still-functioning 1607 brewery; they must be doing something right for 400 years! Then, by way of contrast, I came upon an old Romanesque church still in use. It's far simpler than the cathedral I spotted in the town square, with the musty smell of the centuries. It has a small reliquary containing a piece of a garment said to belong to Peter – or Paul – the brochure suggests they're not quite sure which.

But now, the best known of Euroburg's sights. I returned along the canal and the piers to the shore opposite Old Town. Here, there are low white, chalky cliffs that serve as plant holders for old pines, ash, and chestnut trees in tailored gardens. Above them is the old postcard castle, partially restored after the war (and other wars) with skinny turrets and parapets. It's better known for the number of times its walls were breeched than for the few occasions it actually repelled its assailants. My guidebook says it had two functions, to house the Count and his family (generations thereof) and to loom over the toll house below to ensure that all passing boats fed the coffers of the town and the Count. The toll house still stands on the canal's edge, now a tourist information bureau. The book describes the castle's history as "…built, burned, built, destroyed, remodeled, bombed, and rebuilt." A sad history in fairyland. One can wander around and inside its shell now, with only the old servants' quarters still fully intact, and housing the current inheritors of the Count's mantle.

Beyond the castle and an old residential area is a huge public park called the Grand Park, like many we've seen in these cities: paths, ponds, picnic areas, gardens, gazebos, soccer pitches, and the usual water birds being chased by the usual children and cats. I spent some time at a huge chess board etched into the pavement, each square measuring 12x12 inches and the chess pieces up to two feet tall. I watched as a teenager wiped out a series of adult opponents, making each move immediately after his opponent took up to a minute for each of his moves. This was clearly the boy's turf.

One other item deserves notice. On the east side of the Grand Park there is a huge – and I mean *huge* – mound that looks artificial. And so it is. As I reached it, I came upon a series of plaques dedicated to various categories of people. The mound is called Bomber Mountain, and consists of all the detritus from the war-time shelling and bombing that could not be used in rebuilding the city. It was all dumped here as an anti-war memorial. It towers perhaps a hundred feet above the garden, mirroring the castle turrets to the south with an observation tower at the top. I didn't go up – too high for these old legs – but as a memorial it's fully as impressive as the bombed out cathedrals allowed to remain, as is, that we saw in Berlin and Hamburg. Good for the Euroburgers.

Ok, love, that's the end of the tourist report. I'll finish off this letter and leave it at the hotel desk. I'm off this afternoon for my first meeting with Martin's group. I'm going to limit myself to maybe three items, so as not to overwhelm them with too much literature or too many details. It'll be interesting to meet the other members and gauge their reactions – especially concerning the worker assault. I'll try to call you tonight and provide some overview.

Cheers — (your "American Consultant"!)

The afternoon staff meeting was far more orderly, and rapid, than the consultant had expected. After brief introductions, Keller turned the meeting over to the consultant and participated only occasionally. Topic number one was the assault, and the discussion allowed him to gauge some staff characteristics. Alexander was the spokesman for his group, reiterating their intention to continue serving the Zealots while gathering data the project required. The payoff, for him, was money in Zealot pockets. Abu, still with an ear bandage, but with his red colors already fading to blues and grays, seemed more upset at himself than at his Smokes assailants. The incident was closed, in his mind. He chuckled as Liz commented that he looked better in pastels than bright colors.

The addition of Dirk to the Heinrich and Liz duo seemed fine to the consultant. Dirk appeared to have a youthful enthusiasm without any of the repressed anger that could be read into Heinrich's demeanor. The consultant worried more about Heinrich's seeming self-certainty and pride; was it adequately based in experience in the field? As to Conrad, there was more than met the eye. He was a tall, blond, young Swede seemingly out of place in a world of Arab Muslim gangs. What was his interest, the consultant wondered; he also wondered about what were clearly tattoo removal scars on Conrad's arms and neck, certainly unusual for Swedish youth.

In any case, the assault issue was soon set aside, but it was used to introduce the consultant's first topic. Where was the police expertise in the group? (Keller's pipe was suddenly discarded as he leaned forward on this question. He had not anticipated it). The consultant knew this would be a bomb. Street workers don't like or trust cops. Many gang researchers don't value police data. And police generally reciprocate these views.

"But why do we need the police," came the chorus. The answers were several.

1. In case of emergency, such as Abu's assault, a responsive cop can be a blessing.

2. The project eventually may want access to police information and data on gangs and their members. A cop assigned as liaison to the project could prove invaluable.

3. The police are the only agency in an area with a city-wide view of gang activity. All other agencies only know their own jurisdictional areas.

4. A knowledgeable officer can provide understanding about the local laws, how offenses are classified, how they are handled.

5. Police offense data, when combined with youth survey and other ethnographic reports, can provide better triangulation on what's going on in delinquent and criminal activity. Each source has biases; they need the corrective of other sources.

6. Police data have their own errors and holes. One needs familiarity with their handling in order to use them most effectively.

"All right," Keller broke in, "I find the proposal worth our attention. We'll discuss it later, and see how best to approach it. What's next?" Whatever questions the staff members had would be handled internally, but a look around the room suggested there would be problems, Liz and Magda probably excepted.

Next was the consultant's promise to provide citations to European gang research studies involving Muslim groups. He mentioned reports involving Algerians in France, Pakistanis in England and Norway, Moroccans in the Netherlands, and Turks in Germany. Magda offered to gather the reports and get copies for everyone to review.

Last on the consultant's list for the day was a copy of the STAGE gang research proposal submitted to the E.U. for funding in 2007. A brief review, to be expanded later, included the following.

STAGE was a consortium proposal put together by the research team of Juanjo Medina and Judith Aldridge at the University of Manchester, with heavy consultation from principal members of the Eurogang Program. If funded, it would be the first prospective, multi-site, multi-method gang project in Europe, and the ultimate aim of the Eurogang Program as expounded ten years previously (see Maxson in Klein et al., *The Eurogang Paradox*).

STAGE was designed for implementation in nine countries simultaneously over a four-year period. Five sites, in Manchester, Toulouse, Amsterdam, Barcelona, and Genoa, would employ four Eurogang instrument protocols: experts survey, youth survey, ethnographic guidelines, and administrative data collection. Four sites, in Sarajevo, Tallinn, Bucharest, and Dublin would do all but the resource-heavy ethnography. All design issues – sampling procedures, numbers of cases, access procedures, community engagement and feedback, statistical analysis procedures and the like would be coordinated and as identical as possible to yield maximum comparability and generalizability of the findings. Led and coordinated by Manchester, this broad, inclusive project would be the first of its kind and a beacon for future projects, such as the Euroburg Project, and Euroburg could "steal" from STAGE to determine much of its own procedures.

It is fair to say that Keller's team, and Keller no less than the others, were taken aback by this description. Suddenly they were far more "legitimate" than before, part of a much larger whole than they knew, not just a group on the make but an independent cog in a well-oiled machine. Keller and Magda, in particular, sensed how the STAGE proposal would make their tasks so much easier. Now they not only had fully prepared research instruments, thanks to Eurogang, but also well-considered decisions on how the whole package of the project could be handled. And, as Keller told his group, "We can have research friends all over the continent. We'll learn so much more this way, and we'll be able to tell the officials of Euroburg just where they fit in a far more important context. By God, that's when we'll give Patrick van der Waal his real story!" he turned to his American consultant and said, "What, my dear friend, would be your most desired brand of Scotch to be delivered to your hotel?"

16. Sgt. André Mellers Joins Up

It took less than a week for police liaison arrangements to be made, following the briefest possible staff discussion. Prof. Martin Keller had already made his decision. Keller spoke with the deputy mayor, who spoke with the police chief. The chief instructed the deputy chief to select a liaison officer. The deputy chief told Sergeant André Mellers, head of the gang intelligence unit, that he had been appointed to work with the university team.

This did not make Mellers a happy camper. He was not comfortable with university "types" as he called them, and had little tolerance for street workers who molly-coddled gang members (he called the members "gangsters"). But orders are orders, and the seargeant would do his minimal best.

The first step was to invite his new superior to see Euroburg as his officers saw it. A ride-along was arranged. Prof. Keller and his American consultant would spend the night watch on Friday with a patrol unit. After signing legal waivers to absolve the police department of any responsibility should the passengers sustain "injury or death," the two university types joined two officers in a police van – a Volkswagen mini-bus large enough for four officers and two suspects behind wire mesh. This was a radio unit as well as a riot unit with shotgun and tear gas. "Our job is to protect you," said the driver, adding "it's Friday night – anything can happen on crime night." Keller and the consultant were not impressed; both had been on ride-alongs over the years, and had largely been bored by the action. More pertinent was understanding the officers' perspectives.

The cruise started in the late afternoon, with the following notes jotted down by Keller:

"1. Cruise of the small red light district: about 30 windows, but fewer than half of them occupied in the late afternoon.

2. Car driving incorrectly; a Citroën, so probably Frenchmen seeking hash. Stop, do vehicle check, send them on their way.

3. Check out large American car; suspect pimp driver. Nothing.

4. Cruise of downtown disco area.

5. Eighty mile-per-hour drive on the western highway to no visible purpose. Showing off?

6. Call to minor traffic accident.

7. Call to pick up homeless female mental patient, transport to station. Half hour for coffee.

8. Call to pick up car-booster and his loot (2 radios and clothing). Transport to station. Another coffee break.

9. Stop two wrong-way drivers in pedestrian mall area.

10. Stop motorbike with helmetless driver. Citation. A big day on the farm, on crime night."

But near the end of the shift came word that the Euroburg soccer team had defeated a team from Wales in the semi-finals of the Continental League. The winning goal had been scored, the police radio reported, by an Iraqi refugee from the Village. "Refugee?" queried the police driver; "More likely a recruit." The radio crackled again that people were pouring out into the streets in celebration. The ride-along unit was ordered to cruise the Middle East area and watch for conflict between Fort Araby and the Village.

"Oh hell," said the second officer to the passengers. "We never go there. I don't like this."

"Why," from the consultant.

"These people don't like us, don't respect us or any authority. They want to handle things their own way, and that's fine with me. One of our younger officers got badly beaten trying to help the victim of a group assault. They don't want us; we don't go in there."

But as the car moved north toward the Middle East, it had to slow to a crawl to weave through jubilant crowds waving the regional orange and blue flags, and not a few beer cans as well. The spirit was so catching, the driver said, "What the hell, let's penetrate right between the Fort and the Village and make like fans." They did, and met only joyous Arabs, young and old, clapping and singing. They saw no conflicts, no ugliness as the four of them gave thumbs up and V for victory signals. You couldn't tell a Moroccan from a Turk, a Smoke from a Zealot. Said the consultant to his friend Martin; "You see: group process trumps ethnicity and neighborhood. Maybe soccer is your mayor's answer, and he can take back your research money." Keller was not overly amused.

The second step was to work toward access to police data. Keller sent Heinrich and Liz to meet with their newest friend and colleague, André Mellers. This was handy, as the juvenile and gang units were located near the subway station of the Akbar Café and the Middle East. Juvenile and gang records were housed here, not at the major police station downtown. The building's location near the Akbar Café is a bit ironic. Until the mid-14th century, it had been a synagogue. When the Jews were killed and expelled during the black plague, it became a small convent for 300 years, and then a city jail, followed by a fire station. In the 1960s, the police juvenile unit took it over, with space given to the new gang unit in 2001. Almost unnoticed by visitors to the units, but photographed by the American consultant during the ride-along, were two carved Jewish stars on the outside front wall to the right and left of the entrance, two stories up. Did the Muslim suspects notice, on their way into police interrogation?

Certainly Heinrich and Liz did not as they followed André Mellers up the steps and into the first floor squad room of the gang unit. For the next hour, André and two other gang officers displayed their intelligence wares. There were maps with pins showing the location of gang-related crime incidents. There were half a dozen thick file folders (not opened for Heinrich and Liz) for youth groups labeled street gangs by André's unit, each containing police records of contacts, citations, arrest, and convictions, along with street names, addresses, known associates, auto and motor scooter descriptions and licenses, tattoos and photos, and more. Liz asked how many names were in the Smokes folder. The answer "over 100" shocked them both; she and Hein had identified fewer than 20 to date.

Asked what kinds of crimes were recorded in the files, André responded with a gang-stereotypic list: murders and attempted murders, assaults, robberies, witness intimidation, auto thefts, felony thefts, arson, and drug sales or possession for sale. Heinrich noted to himself that these were all serious offenses, whereas most things he was hearing about were minor thefts, fights, trespasses, joy-riding, graffiti, under-age drinking, minor drug use and other low felony or misdemeanor offenses. Why weren't these recorded, he wondered, while being happy at the same time that they weren't.

But the biggest surprise came when André went to one of several wall draperies and drew one open. Above a large board was the word Smokes, and below that a number of sets of photos – mostly mug shots – connected in a series of networks. These were, André explained, "crime cliques" or groups of offenders arrested together or just observed together. Smokes arrested alone were not included so André referred to the cliqued-up members as the hardcore Smokes. These, he said, were the primary targets for arrest and conviction. Heinrich and Liz, having agreed beforehand not to reveal any police intelligence without prior approval, felt overwhelmed and frustrated. How correct was this intelligence? How legally was it used? How could it be incorporated into the project without revealing identities? They asked to set up a meeting with André and the professor on such issues – and Magda, added Liz. André said in that favorite of all European phrases, "No problem."

Discussion about some of the names known to both the police and the researchers led to some relaxed gossiping: Mustafa, Muhammed H., Kemal, a few of the elders and others. It was André's view that few of them "had all their candles lit." If they were bright, or responsible, or both, they'd be in school, in jobs, and not in trouble. Most of what they did was stupid. He offered the apocryphal story on the internet as an example:

The murderer wore a fake beard, fake mustache, rode a bike, and used a gun. Police obtained a search warrant to look for the murder weapon in the house of the man they suspected of being the murderer. Police didn't find the murder weapon, but did find the following checklist, with each item checkmarked:

- Beard
- Mustache
- Bicycle
- Gun
- Dispose of murder weapon

André and his colleagues absolutely guffawed at the end of his story, and Heinrich lost it. Liz, his minder, could not control him this time.

"Swell; to you guys these kids – gang members, immigrants, however you label them – are nothing but stupid louts. To you, they're just someone to be busted and taken off the streets. What a simple life you lead. There's bad kids and there's your kids, right?"

"Now wait a minute, Heinrich. You're talking to cops, not social workers. Our job is to maintain order, to serve the regular citizens of the city, to protect them against crime. If you want to bleed for criminals, you can, but don't expect us to."

"Yeah," said another officer. "Just about every kid out there in Fort Araby and the Village is a gang member, or an associate member. We're *supposed* to keep tabs on them. And we'll do even better when we finally get all these folders and the clique intelligence computerized. And for the ones you know, you oughta be helping us. For instance, this Mustafa of yours—as far as I'm concerned, he's a violent Smoke, but my partner says he's not really involved and has no serious crimes on his plate these days. And the sergeant doesn't believe Mustafa's an active gang member at all. So you should tell us what you know and we can put Mustafa where he belongs."

It was Liz who broke up the confrontation. "You have about 100 Smokes in your list. But how many gang-age boys are in Fort Araby? I'll bet, between 12 and 20 years of age, there are at least a thousand or even more. That means maybe 10 percent are gang-affiliated. I think you gentlemen and we can work together effectively on getting better information on these youth. You call it intelligence; we call it research data. So let's hold the arguments for now, and we can get together with Prof. Keller to find where we can combine forces. If Heinrich and the sergeant can hold back their anger and their jokes, I'll bet we can do a decent job."

With some grumbling and head-nodding, the party broke up. The lines were drawn, but Liz at least spoke up for a truce. Not such a bad start. In the next few days and discussions with the consultant who had raised the police issue to begin with, several decisions were reached in the team:

1. André Mellers would join the team each week in its regular staff meeting;

2. Magda, with André's help, would develop a police records search and coding scheme, one that would protect confidentiality but also identify co-offenders;

3. Liz and Conrad would be assigned to undertake the records search, under the watchful eye of André;

4. The consultant would get Magda in contact with Cheryl Maxson in California, who had carried out and supervised a number of police record searches in gang projects. Keller would provide financial support for this special consultation;

5. The consultant and the Professor would become "court watchers," carrying out observations of the judicial process in each gang case that the police and prosecutors brought to trial.

The university team and the justice system, however haltingly, were about to join forces in clarifying the nature of the gang problem in Euroburg.

Cop meets author in Euroburg.

17. Background Statement: Gang Crime Data

[Special Comments from the Author]

The American consultant's recommendation to seek advice on extracting and coding offense information from the police records was not just a matter of knowing a particular expert such as Dr. Maxson. It resulted as well from a singular weakness in the Eurogang Program. For all its careful and successful work in developing reliable research instruments, the Program did not produce any protocol or guidelines for collecting archival data. Police and court records, most specifically, did not receive attention in the Eurogang developments.

The reasons for this gap were several, and understandable. European researchers have not shared the enthusiasm for police data often shown by their American colleagues. Some European police departments have not yet publicly admitted they have a gang problem and thus have not developed gang expertise. Many departments have only loosely defined what they mean by gang and gang member, and they have not reached mutual agreements on these terms. Distinguishing between gang-related and nongang crime is as much art and experience as it is law. In many such instances, then, archival

Malcolm W. Klein

data collection could prove fruitless. Euroburg is representative of some cities, however, where police records *can* produce useful gang data. Examples include Stockholm, Oslo, Manchester, Frankfurt, Berlin, Brussels, London, and the Hague. In such cities, it is important to understand what is offered by police data as compared to youth interview data.

Three principal approaches to crime measurement are available. The first, victim surveys, are less appropriate to juvenile crime and also to gang crime which more commonly involves strangers and unknown perpetrators (who, therefore, cannot be described by victims). Victim surveys are not appropriate to most street gang research.

The second approach is the use of "self-report" or admitted crime. School-based, household, or "snowball" interviews and questionnaires ask respondents to report and describe their own illegal behaviors to researchers. Generally, youth have been found to be surprisingly useful reporters on their own behaviors. The now well-known International Self-Report Delinquency (ISRD) instrument has been administered across dozens of countries over the past decade with good reliability and very useful results. The Youth Survey instrument developed by the Eurogang Program employs a shorter variation of the ISRD in its survey protocol.

The third approach is the use of police (and occasionally court) records to assess criminal activity. In more careful departments, the recorded crime data are reliably collected, but comparisons across departments, and in some instances across time, are marred by different and changing definitions and procedures.

Why is it important to get a good fix on youth crime in gang areas? Because it is different. John Pitts, who had earlier reported to one of the Eurogang workshops on non-gang groups in London, has since followed with an extensive report of the opposite, a community that has spawned street gangs. In a 2007 University of Bedfordshire report entitled *Reluctant Gangsters*, Pitts describes the crime in such areas as follows:

1. It is youthful: both victims and perpetrators are young
2. It is implosive: the youth involved are local residents
3. It is repetitive: victims become renewed victims, and often
4. It is symmetrical: victims and perpetrators are much alike
5. It is violent, and visibly so
6. It is underreported to officials
7. In the absence of alternative, pro-social life pathways, youthful offending becomes embedded in the lifestyle, a process that helps create street gangs.

86

Because of this connection between crime characteristics and gang formation, the best measures of youth offending we can muster become critical to understanding street gang formation and persistence. While arguments persist about the validity of self-report versus police measures of crime, a self-report survey applied across jurisdictions yields far more comparable and reliable data than separate sets of police data. In addition, self-report surveys provide vastly more information about the crime perpetrators because surveys can ask about many things not available to the police. Finally, self-report surveys yield far more data – more offenses – because most illegal acts are simply not reported to the police nor are the perpetrators generally known. An early comparison from Brussels, reported in a Eurogang Program study (Vercaigne, 2001) is illustrative. Among 5,000 young people surveyed, about 80 percent of the admitted crimes were never detected. In American data, the figure is usually even greater, especially for minor offenses.

The same study reports that from 40 to 90 percent of offenses are carried out mostly with two or more offenders (depending on the type of offense). This figure would be expected to be even higher among gang members, but if police departments like that in Brussels cannot collect effective information on gang members, then the very nature of gang crime cannot be well discerned from police records to the extent it can from self-report surveys.

Nor does this exhaust the problems in using police gang crime data. For instance, street gang members do not commit crimes at the *same tempo* as each other, nor do they display the *same pattern* of offenses. If police gang intelligence is weak in defining gangs and gang members, weak in determining which are the more and less active members, then such intelligence can be very misleading as to the crime activities of core and fringe members. Further it will be even more so with respect to members less well-known (or not known at all) to the police.

Another problem is that departments, by implicit or very explicit policy, vary in their concern for minor versus major types of offenses. Some departments attempt to record as many gang-related offenses as they can, providing a broad picture of their gangs' criminal activity. Others, as in Euroburg, manifest interest only in the more serious crimes and those thought to be stereotypic or "gang-like." Such departments thus record far fewer offenses, and provide images of gangs as violent, organized, predatory groups. They do so by overlooking half to three-quarters of recordable gang member offenses. Self-report surveys are far less vulnerable to such disparities in depicting gang member activities.

Two crime exaggerations in particular are to be found in police recording systems that concentrate on stereotypic gang offending. One, of course, is violence, where narrower police perspectives yield depictions of "the violent street gang," whereas violent crime usually amounts to 10 percent or less of the offenses committed. It would be more valid to speak of "drinking gangs" or "drug using gangs," or "petty theft gangs" or "disturbing the peace gangs" since these activities are far more common than violence.

A recent summary of violence patterns reported in Eurogang Program reports (Klein, Weerman, and Thornberry, 2007) included the following:

1. Levels of violence are generally well below those reported in American studies (although considerable variance exists);

2. Gun violence is also far less common;

3. Motives for European street gang violence are less often related to territoriality than to ethnically-based revenge, group identity and status, and crime support;

4. Violence victims are determined in large part by violence motives, i.e., victimization tends to be rational, not "random" or "senseless" as is often reported in the press.

The second exaggeration, less common but equally misleading in forming public opinion and policy, is the depiction of street gangs as drug trafficking groups or even drug cartels, where gang organizations and the drug selling patterns go hand in hand. There are "drug gangs," of course, but by and large street gang organization is far too loose and changing to produce effective drug trafficking conspiracies. Again, self-report surveys explode the myths of violent gangs and drug trafficking gangs.

Another problem relates directly to the patterns of crimes committed by street gangs like Euroburg's Smokes and Zealots. Most members live on the outskirts of European cities like Euroburg. Their "gang stereotypic" crimes are more likely to be seen in their residential areas: graffiti, fighting, drug use and sales are more local. But when they go downtown, a higher proportion of crimes will be property crimes: theft, robberies, smash-and-grab burglaries, vandalism, and the like. If the police concentrate on their gang surveillance in one area more than another, crime reports will reflect *police* patterns, not just gang patterns. Remember what we have learned about the Euroburg police – they don't like to patrol in Fort Araby and the Village.

Given all this, then why do we bother with police data? If we know a department's gang intelligence is poor, we shouldn't bother for research purposes. However, if the intelligence is good – note how shocked were Heinrich and Liz at what André Mellers showed them – then police data can fill in holes and provide alternative perspectives. Further, they are city-wide, which ethnographic data are not and survey data often are not.

But most important perhaps, is the simple fact that police reports of crime and very specifically *gang* crime, are a major factor in driving public opinion and public policy (often mirrored in press reports like those of Patrick van der Waal). Self-report survey data seldom if ever penetrate public consciousness. Having both police and self-report crime information puts the researcher in a unique position to inform colleagues and the public alike why research analysis can inform both science and policy.

18. The Eurogang Program

While the American consultant was still in town, Keller wanted him to provide an overview of the Eurogang Program for the full project team. Most particularly he wanted the non-university members to have a feeling for how the Euroburg street gang project fit into "the larger intellectual context" as he phrased it. In particular, he wanted the Zealot workers Alexander, Muzafer, and Abu to see how their work in the field would contribute beyond their contributions to the gang members. And he wanted Sgt. Mellers to think beyond his law enforcement goals to the broader goals of adding to knowledge about street gangs generally.

To these ends, he asked the consultant to take over the next team meeting "I'd like us all to hear two things," he opened. "First give us a sense for the progress and development of the program as a whole. Then, if you will, I'd like you to share with us why *you* are such a fan of the program. What does it mean to you, personally; share with us your passion for it. I've learned over the past few weeks that you really do have such a passion."

"All right," responded the consultant, "I accept the challenge, Martin; although I may have some problems with the passion part of it. Incidentally," he said as he looked in particular toward the four students, "I have addressed Professor Keller as 'Martin' for all my days here, but I note that the rest of you all address him as 'Professor.' This is not so common in the states; would any of you think about or consider addressing him as 'Martin'?" There was a cacophony of "Oh no"s, "we couldn't"s, and embarrassed gasps around the conference room. If one had looked at Keller, there would have been a bemused smile. And if one had looked at Magda, a picture of suppressed humor might have been seen. André Mellers looked around in sheer puzzlement. "No, I guess not," concluded the consultant; "different academic cultures, I guess. OK, I'll move on to the program." Whereupon, a rather didactic lecture proceeded, with the following components.

The starting point was during two sabbatical leaves the consultant and his wife spent in Stockholm, he at the National Council on Crime Prevention and Stockholm University, she at the Karolinska Institute in what is now the Department of Epidemiology. They had been alerted to possible street gang developments in Sweden and several other countries, and undertook a brief traveling survey to assess the situation. In Zurich, Berlin, Stuttgart, Frankfurt, London, Manchester, Amsterdam, and The Hague, public officials or scholars reported the presence of street gang activity. Other similar reports soon came in from Russia, Norway, Denmark, Belgium, France, and Slovenia, along with denials from others in Belgium, England, Finland, Italy, and Spain.

There was reason enough to convene a small group of interested researchers, and after two preliminary meetings, a government funded workshop was held in Germany. In a string of nine workshops to date, several have been pivotal - Schmitten, Oslo, Albany, and Onati. The Schmitten workshop in 1998 brought together for the first time established American gang researchers with a group of relatively new European scholars undertaking group and gang research in response to the developments since the mid-1980s.

Some of the Europeans were concerned that gang research – even using the term "gang" – could trigger a moral panic in some countries, creating the very phenomenon under study. A few others denied that their cities had a gang problem because none of their youth groups resembled the media depictions of American street gangs – large, territorial, violent, hierarchically organized criminal groups like the Latin Kings or Black Gangster Disciples of Chicago, or the Crips and Bloods of Los Angeles. It fell to the American workshop participants to spell out what has come to be known as "The Eurogang Paradox." The paradox is that Europe was said not to have street gangs because their groups didn't resemble those "Westside Story" stereotypes of American street gangs, yet most American gangs as well did not (and do not) fit that stereotype.

Once the paradox was spelled out and illustrated by the American researchers, it allowed the Europeans to rethink some of their youth groups, and see that they did indeed resemble a large portion of American gangs.

The Schmitten meeting was thus able to consider gang and nongang group studies from both continents, leading in turn to the first published book produced under the Eurogang Program (Klein et al., 2001).

The second workshop, in Oslo, was equally pivotal to the rapidly growing program. In it, a series of working groups were established to provide technical structure and progress for the program. The first of these, crucial to each of the others, was the definitions working group which, over several years, finally established the consensus Eurogang definition, that "a street gang is any durable street-oriented youth group whose involvement in illegal behavior is part of its group identity."

This definition was incorporated into the deliberations of the other working groups on (1) the experts survey, (2) the youth survey, (3) the ethnographic guidelines, (4) the city descriptors survey, and (5) the intervention survey. The common definition allowed two forms of comparability by devising operational measures of street gangs: comparability across instruments so that each survey was measuring the same phenomenon, and comparability across gang studies because each instrument could be used in identical form in each study. In other words, the Oslo developments led to the structure of a multi-site, multi-method approach to gang research as demonstrated most recently in the nine-country STAGE proposal developed at the University of Manchester.

The next pivotal workshop of the nine to date was the seventh, held in Albany, New York, just as a second book based on proceedings of the intervening workshops was published (Decker and Weerman, 2005). Three developments were important. First, half of the workshop was devoted not to the instrumentation components of the program but for the first time to a conceptual issue, in this case the nature of violence in European street gangs. This in turn emphasized the need to turn to broader conceptual issues within which to understand European street gang activity and growth. Finally, Albany participants were able to agree that the Eurogang instruments, after translations, pilot research, pre-testing and initial analyses, were ready to be made available broadly. With minimal restrictions, they were entered into an internet web page and now can be accessed and used by serious scholars (as in the case of the Euroburg project).

The eighth workshop, held in Onati, Spain in 2005 was devoted almost exclusively to the broader social contexts of European gangs. The instrumentation phase was over, and the Eurogang Program had moved into a second major phase. Migration and ethnicity were the focus of papers and discussions in Onati, resulting in the third published volume (van Gemert, Peterson, and Lien, 2008). As it happens, this expansion into looking at the growing and troublesome immigration issues in Europe was perfectly timed for the decision to undertake the STAGE project. The European Union put out a call in 2007 for proposals for research on "socially excluded youth." If funded, the proposal for comparative gang research in nine countries would move the Eurogang Program to a third and long-desired phase of multi-site, multi-method research (Maxson, 2001).

At this point, the American called for a break in the lecture, and Magda was already prepared with coffee, tea, and biscuits. "Before I move on," said the consultant, "I want to stress my hope that all the students, and others so inclined, read and consider carefully the three Eurogang volumes I mentioned today. For people just getting into the issues of street gang knowledge, like Alexander, Muzafer, and Abu, I've written a short introduction called *Chasing After Street Gangs* (2007) that might prove helpful. Finally, because I've spent so much time with police officers in gang units, I've written a special, half-fictional work called *Gang Cop* (2004). I'm asking Magda to get this for you, André, but as you read it keep in mind that the gang cop protagonist is a stereotype, not someone as forward thinking as you appear to be." Chuckles around the room eased the tension for the sergeant.

Questions and answers followed for a while, until Keller repeated his second request: "Let's hear about your passions, my friend. You've been involved in the Eurogang Program for something like ten years now; what keeps you going?"

"I suppose," was the reply, "some combination of pride, stubbornness, intellectual curiosity, my original training as a social psychologist which includes an interest in what makes groups tick, and the continuing pleasure my wife and I get from traveling about Europe. Let's take the group and travel interests as more personal but less relevant to your team. That leaves me with several more interests, or passions if you insist on labeling them as such, Martin. I doubt that I have many colleagues who would use my name and passion in the same sentence.

"For one thing, I like the sheer enormity of the program. We've been involved in nine workshops and numbers of other meetings at the A.S.C. and the E.S.C. We've engaged over 150 – now it's close to 200 – colleagues in over 50 cities in 21 European countries to date. And this has been accomplished with a minimum of state and foundation funding. So many people, so much volunteered time, and so much stability from a core group of steering committee and working group members means other people have some 'passion' as well.

"Second, as an American 'gangster' I've had a chance to broaden my perspectives and knowledge to an unusual extent. I had a couple of trips to China many years ago that did the same thing for me. You can come to some excitement about your own ideas if you get to test them out, modify them, and improve them through exposure to other intellectual climates. Maybe 'excitement' fits my feelings more properly than 'passion'.

"Third, I've had a superb opportunity to spread the word about group processes and gang structure or types that most scholars *and* practitioners tend to overlook. Most street gang work focuses on individual gang members or on broad social institutions, but seldom on the close-in triggers of gang development and activity that one sees with a focus on the gang as a group. I'm excited about getting people to remember that gangs are not merely collections of individuals; they are *groups*, with special group qualities.

"Finally, I'm becoming more interested if not passionate about having people pay more attention to community issues in the gang area. The Eurogang Program's second phase, with current emphasis on migration and ethnicity, is a step in this direction. But you know, street gangs don't appear out of thin air. They are spawned within communities and neighborhoods, they are reinforced there to become durable groups, and eventually it is those same communities that must hold a central power in controlling the gang problem. Individual change is inefficient and beyond our resources. Law enforcement can apply band aids and constraints, but it can't undo the harms already done. I'm passionate, then, about the possibilities for local, community prevention and control. Different phrases are used: local social control, community empowerment, social efficacy, each being a variation on the major theme. We need to spend more time understanding the theme, and then learning how to use it. Maybe the Eurogang Program can move to this; maybe your Euroburg project can be a part of this direction. Then you too can feel some of my excitement."

And with that, the team meeting should have ended, and Keller signaled as much by standing up, putting his pipe away, reaching out to shake his American friend's hand, and moving toward the door. But he had not become Sgt. André Mellers' leader, not yet. "That's all fine and good for researchers," he announced, "but my job is to protect and serve the public – the God-fearing, law-abiding public. I do that through gathering gang intelligence and arresting gang members. I can't arrest groups, and I sure as hell can't arrest communities. I'd like to see you people have some excitement, some passion, about what it is I and my people do. Anyone care to spend some time out there with me?"

Keller was astounded by this break in his control, but the consultant immediately responded: "Count me in. Let's go for a drive in your town tomorrow. Anyone else?"

19. André's Streets

"I don't know what we'll find," announced the sergeant, "but let's get out on the streets." It was the morning following his pronouncement about his cop's role. Keller, Liz, and the American consultant met him at the institute both to assuage him and get him further connected to their areas of research. He, of course, felt that today *he* was the teacher.

They entered his unmarked car (well-known, of course, to street-wise gang members, pimps, prostitutes, and drug dealers who could spot it a block away). They drove first to the town square where some sort of public affair was being prepared, but it was to the rear of St. Agnes Cathedral that André went. Under the shelter of the holy house was a half-block red light district. None of the windows were open for business yet this morning, but André pointed out several lounging pimps and mustachioed dealers – "Turkish," he noted. Their runners would be the ones without the mustaches. Two uniformed officers were watching from down the street: "We'd rather be around and visible to deter any serious action. No point in just arresting guys who'll be back here in an hour. So now let's keep going to church," he said as he drove on to the Roman museum and a reconstructed, very old chapel at its entrance. "Fourteenth century is what they claim, but look who's claiming it as their territory." He pointed to a small group of punkers with flaming, stand-up hair. "They don't give us much trouble, but we have to keep moving them along so they don't scare away our bread-and-butter tourists."

The good sergeant was beginning to enjoy himself; the lessons were out in the street, highly visible to his new "students." They drove on to the canal, where André pointed out two small motor launches with city insignia. "Our water police," he explained. "Sometimes cars, even buses go in and our guys have to pull folks out. Drunken bicyclists, too. Our guys also check out polluters, control boat traffic and drunken helmsmen and so on. If a boat ties up at a pier and gets a lot of visitors, the water police and out narcotics officers will surveil them, maybe bust them or move them out to the river and the next town."

They parked by the canal – illegally – and walked back up to the town square. Now the affair had taken shape: a political rally of sorts, with separate booths for each candidate or his or her party. Signs, balloons, small bands, and most of all, beer by the keg. It's free, André noted: "Our candidate provides the best beer, so vote for us. Of course, by noon time our guys have to go in and start pulling out the drunks; politics and police, working together," he sneered.

It started to rain – a cold mist, really, signalling entry into the fall season – so they returned to the car and drove out to the Middle East. At the open market in the Village, vendors were closing down their stalls as mist, wind, and disappearing shoppers forced a pull back. All but the butcher's display, where lamb and fowl were still being chopped and hung. Our observers stand terrified before a tall, slender butcher who wielded his meat cleaver like a surgeon's knife – first delicate and precise, then full of flourishes and circular sweeps, never missing his target. Liz pointed to his left hand holding those meat targets; he was missing four fingers on that hand. He had once not been so deft!

André pointed out some gang graffiti on several stall walls, some in Arabic and some in block letters : "Zealots," "Muslims Rule." "We started an anti-graffiti campaign downtown," he reported. "If a Zealot sign, or a Smokes sign, or a Skinhead symbol showed up, no matter where it was we forced the next arrestees to go with brushes and paint thinner to clean it off. There's an example," he said turning to the American, "where we *do* use the group structure against the gang."

He then pointed to two young males who were helping close some stalls. André identified them as two of Alexander's "so-called reformed gangsters" who gave talks in local schools about the evils of drug use. "One of them we know is still a user, and we're watching the other one, too. These guys don't reform, they just play at it. Most gang members keep their gang mentality for life. We've checked out Alexander and Abu and Muzafer and they're clean as far as we can tell. Otherwise I wouldn't work with them." He then looked at Liz, winked, and said "But I haven't checked out this young lady yet." Liz did not wink back, or smile, but only heaved a sigh of resignation.

Back in the car, they drove a bit west, past Fort Araby. André pointed to the spot where "one of our young officers tried to break up a gang assault and got beat all to hell for his effort. This is not a healthy place for rookie cops." They passed on without entering the Fort and returned to the station, near the Akbar Café, where André's gang unit was housed, separate from and independent of all other police supervision (along with the juvenile division).

As they entered the station, two young boys were being led to the temporary lock-up in the back while juvenile officers made obscene remarks and gestures in their direction. It turned out they had been arrested for molesting some girls in a grade school locker room. The gestures were quite explicit. Liz turned to André as if he might intervene, but he showed no interest or concern; he was not in the juvenile division. They moved on to André's squad room where he showed them the gang folders and his hardcore crime cliques structures. He was in his element, making his case, after a good tour of criminal Euroburg as he knew it. But Liz wasn't buying it. Don't wink at me, fella, was her attitude.

"You really think gang members can't reform, that they're in it for good?"

"Well," he answered, "pretty much all the ones I've known, yes."

"Ok, well how about this? You told Heinrich and me there were over a hundred Smokes right now, right? Let's figure they've been in Fort Araby for at least 15 years, maybe twenty. So as each generation grows older, younger ones have to come in to replace them, right? So a typical Smoke stays active maybe five years, OK? So every five years, a new hundred have joined; over 20 years, that's 400 new members, right? But you say there are about a hundred members; where have the other 300 gone, Sergeant? Why aren't you overwhelmed by 400 Smokes?"

Liz, the data hound, had emerged. Don't wink at her, fella! André was forced to retreat. Yes, there probably had been that many over 20 years. He didn't mean they were all still fighting and spraying graffiti and hassling the tourists downtown. But a lot of them were still "affiliated," he said. They weren't choir boys or rug carriers for the imams! "And anyway," he added, "today you saw what the Euroburg the police have to deal with; one hundred or four hundred, it doesn't matter that much."

This was the entry point for the consultant. He, too, wanted to test André's understanding. "I really appreciate that you showed us what you did. Every city I've ever visited has its underside, and I know what you deal with. But sometimes we can put a different face on what we see. I made some mental notes this morning about how thinking about group process and structure can relate to the police role. You yourself, gave one example, making the gang responsible for the individual graffiti writer's actions. But let's turn that around, Sergeant. Put yourself in the gang's mental state. Are they likely to feel remorse for their member's action, or personally responsible for his reform? Are they likely to declare a moratorium against the use of graffiti? Or isn't it more likely that they're going to resent what you've done, that they're going to feel even more alienated and dependent on each other, that writing graffiti may come to symbolize their stance as the whipping boys of the police, of authorities generally?"

André was about to respond – his fellow officers, his audience in the squad room, were counting on him, but the American held up his hand and continued. "Liz made the point, also, at least by implication. If we treat current gang members as unreformable, won't we continue to respond to them in ways that confirm that expectation, that label, which then becomes a self-fulfilling prophecy. If we have to 'check out' people like Alexander and Muzafer and Abu, aren't we inviting the stereotypes that all Middle Eastern young people are gang prone or somehow suspect, and won't this reinforce their in-group feeling and alienation from the rest of us? If we hassle gang 'leaders' like the hardcore clique members you have on your wall, don't we confirm their status? Don't we increase the cohesive feelings in their gang? And Seargeant, if we make it obvious by avoiding Fort Araby that it is a dangerous place, aren't we confirming that idea? Even the police won't go in there? What does that tell the Smokes about their power as a group?

"Now I grant you, we can't stop before every move in the streets to think about what the consequences for group processes and structure might be. But I think we can get into a mindset that tries to create strategies to avoid strengthening gang cohesiveness and that stress individualism – that is, responding to gang members as single individuals, as if they didn't have gang monikers and didn't act for the group but only for themselves. Right now, I'll bet you and your fellow officers here go out as gang cops, thinking in *gang* terms and looking for *gang*-related behavior. But the laws you uphold apply well to *individuals*. Could you go out into the gang world and try to think more in individual terms? You'd get just as many arrests, and just as many convictions, without inadvertently strengthening gang members' bonds to each other. I can tell you this – research strongly suggests that is a fruitful way to go. We could test this out, with your help, in Prof. Keller's project. Then Liz could get off your back!"

Only the officers themselves can know what the ensuing conversation was like in the squad room that afternoon. But André was sufficiently intrigued and challenged that he took the subway back to town with his research companions. Two incidents lightened the day. They entered the subway without punching tickets – a police prerogative that is not to be passed on to friends. As they approached the stop near the central police station, they saw two transit officers checking fare punches and heading their way. André motioned his guests out the door – they would await the next train. Liz asked what André would have done if the transit cops had reached them. "I'd tell them you were in my custody for fare dodging and I'd flash my badge and tell them we are going to the central station. No problem."

After they entered the next train for the short trip to the railway station, they emerged and went through the tunnel to the main waiting room. There they spied a group of six gang-attired Muslim boys huddled in a corner, watching all the action going by. With them were Heinrich and Dirk; Dirk was actually taking notes of some sort as the boys talked. The ethnography of the Smokes was under way, and even André had to smile and turn his back to the gathering. Keller stuck his pipe in his mouth. Liz mimicked him with her finger, while André and the consultant followed them out to the street. Time for lunch in Old Town. Time for the American to prepare for the next few days with the Eurogang instruments.

20. Ethnographic Guidelines

The next morning brought steady rain, a good day to huddle in the conference room. With the exception of André, everyone was present for an overview of field research. André had e-mailed that new intelligence leads connected some of Abu's assaulters with those who had beaten up the young officer earlier at Fort Araby. Following these leads easily took precedence over listening to how researchers would work the streets.

Keller opened the proceedings by passing out copies of the Eurogang protocol for ethnographic guidelines. He read aloud from its introduction:

> The strength of research in the ethnographic tradition is its flexibility. This flexibility is necessary, as research in practice may bring up unexpected obstacles and unforeseen topical imperatives. But also, cross-gang and cross-site comparisons will be greatly facilitated by including a set of required or strongly recommended components.

The professor then pointed out that the Euroburg project had already demonstrated the need for flexibility in studying the two gangs identified so far, because of how the two field teams had developed. The Smokes team of Heinrich, Liz, and Dirk had come to the field from the outside, necessitating a period of preliminary observation, establishing contacts, and building rapport with gang members. They were native Europeans, not Arab or Muslim, and would always face problems of confidence and trust. The threats to Heinrich were an example of the kinds of obstacles the guidelines suggested.

By contrast, the Zealot team of Alexander, Muzafer, and Abu was an "inside team," already part of the culture and already established prior to the research. An obstacle existed for them as well, turning their advocacy roles into part-time research roles. There was certain to be some ambivalence about that process, but at least their acceptance in the gang culture was far advanced over that of the Smokes team.

The advantage of this flexibility, Keller noted, was also a challenge for all of them; two different kinds of gang access and acceptability could yield different sorts of data due not to gang differences but to research differences. "We all have to keep alert to this; Magda and I in particular will keep testing out your reports to understand why differences may appear. Your field notes and written summaries will have to be complete enough and clear about your data sources, so that we can deal with the two different situations. Meanwhile, Magda will be charged with developing a reliable coding system for recording your data and making it quantifiable into the categories suggested by the Eurogang Program's Guidelines."

It was then the consultant's turn to review the ethnographic guidelines. First, he suggested they bring in Frank van Gemert from Amsterdam for consultation. Van Gemert had been one of the co-chairs of the Eurogang working group on the ethnographic guidelines, along with Jody Miller from the U.S., and had extensive experience with Moroccan immigrant groups in particular. Keller and Dirk had met with van Gemert during the summer, and agreed that bringing him into Euroburg was a fine idea. "Should have thought of that myself," said Keller. "And remember that Magda has already collected for us eight articles using gang ethnographies in six different countries."

The consultant next spoke briefly about what he called "the spirit and the art" of ethnography. Typically, ethnographers prefer field work that is unfettered with prior hypotheses or assumptions of what they will find. Their job goes well beyond simple observations and descriptions, regardless of how systematic those are. They need to get inside the culture of the group being studied – its values, social mores and institutions, and the meanings it ascribes to the components of its world. This is as much cultural immersion as it is external investigation. Ethnographers are more willing than the rest of us to suspend their own moral judgments in learning about the cultures of other groups. "As an example, just think of the differences that may arise, under these circumstances, when you talk about your gangs with Sgt. Mellers. The kind of 'cultural relativism' I'm describing would not be likely to warm his judgmental heart." Put this way, everyone in the room could readily grasp some of the truly inherent problems of collaboration between gang workers and gang cops.

The consultant then reviewed four points he had chosen the night before to emphasize in this meeting. First, the guidelines (and the youth survey) were built on a consensus among the Eurogang researchers about what topics were most important to be measured. Most important were the variables that operationalize the Eurogang definition of street gangs: durability, street orientation, youthfulness, and illegal behavior as part of the group's identity. Other important measures include the characteristics of the group structure in order to assess gang types, and measures of the level and types of offending engaged in by group members. The critical topics to be assessed during the ethnographic study of each gang are listed in the guidelines on the fourth and fifth pages: history and local setting, group descriptions, individual gang members, and gang culture. These are followed on the fifth page by other categories. These and yet other issues may be measured, time permitting, so long as the four critical areas are fully covered. Page three of the guidelines also discusses four methods to be employed: participant observation, semi-structured interviews, examination of key events, and interviews with non-gang community members. The consultant again emphasized to the Euroburg team that use of the Eurogang instruments – in this case, the ethnographic guidelines – necessitated using all four methods and gathering data at least on the four categories of variables.

Second, the consultant reminded the team that, of all the instruments, the ethnography and the youth survey went hand in hand. The variables in the guidelines also appear as items in the youth survey to insure comparability. Failure in either case weakens the value of the other. To this end special attention to sampling issues in both methods was pivotal and would have to be discussed before launching the full study.

Third, and in the same spirit, ethnography and survey researchers would have to plan together to assure collection of comparable data. To that end, the final section of the ethnographic guidelines lists questions to be answered about each gang on a brief face sheet that can be easily coded by project staff to make cross-gang comparability an easy affair (and thus cross-city comparability as well).

The consultant's fourth point was of a different order, yet crucial to a team effort involving field work. It is vital, he said, that field workers report on ethical incidents and issues to their superiors, in this case either Prof. Keller or Magda. Such issues cannot be ignored, he emphasized, whether or not they appear to call for some response. The decision about responding *must* be made in concert with the team leaders. The nature of ethical solutions, and feelings about them, are relevant to morality, to political considerations, and to the quality of the research. The threats to Heinrich, the assault on Abu, access to and use of André's clique structure data, and Liz's problems of access to the Muslim gangs and girls were cited as examples. Then the consultant listed some past experiences from his own earlier projects to show how pervasive and varied were the issues that might appear:

"1) A group of five were being sought by the police on assault charges. I was with them when we learned of this. Should I have ignored the issues, or turned them in? I finally persuaded them to go with me to the police station, in the safety of my company to gain whatever credit they might get from showing up instead of being hunted down. The result was that four of them went with me and received decent treatment from the police. The fifth bolted, and was eventually captured in a violent confrontation.

"2) In an interview, one of my research assistants learned of a homicide which the respondent admitted he had committed. She informed me immediately, and we discussed in our group how to respond. We then sought consultation from the Ethics Committee of the American Psychological Association. They responded that they had no guidelines for such a situation, but would we please inform them of our decision so they could include it in their material! Our solution was to keep mum; we couldn't corroborate the admission, and of course had promised anonymity at the beginning of the interview.

"3) One of our street workers – not a researcher – was in a 'mom and pop' store when three gang members he recognized robbed the owners in his presence. Should he have identified the three to the police? His supervisor made him do so, and then transferred him to another location for his own safety.

"4) A field worker, in order to establish rapport with a gang to which he had just been assigned, stalled off all meetings with them until they promised to engage everyone they could to meet with him. His action was very successful, but it also drew new potential gang recruits into his formal program. Should we gain gang access by procedures that might inadvertently build gang size and cohesiveness?

"5) A field worker observed two gang members in a public park displaying weapons – chains, and a club studded with nails. Feeling that his rapport with the group was weak, he decided not to speak with them about either carrying or displaying weapons. Was his judgment correct? Somewhat later, in a gathering within the same gang, this worker's supervisor – a man with considerable self-confidence – saw a member carrying a machete in a sling inside his coat. The supervisor pulled him aside and convinced him to hand over the weapon. Same gang, different approach, different result. How do we determine our approach to gang misbehavior?

"6) During a series of 'snowball' interviews, a respondent agreed to bring in some additional respondents to be interviewed. Each respondent in the study was paid twenty dollars for his participation. One of the snowballed respondents told the interviewer that the youth contacting him was taking half of his payment as a 'fee.' This snowball procedure was our last, desperate attempt to fulfill our own quota of gang respondents. Should we therefore have continued this fee-splitting procedure, or should we have cut off this source of data? We chose the latter approach."

The examples were enough to trigger a discussion lasting well through lunch and beyond. Clear guidelines, it was agreed, are hard to establish ahead of time. Those favored were (1) protection of the field worker, (2) protection of promises to gang members, and (3) protection of victims explicitly cited by gang members as targets of future serious violence. But the onus of decision making was to be in the hands of Keller and Magda who, it was agreed, would be fully informed of any ethical dilemma that developed in the field. Not all ethnographers have such a moral escape hatch.

21. The Experts Survey

The next instrumentation meeting included only Keller, Magda, Liz, and André. The field teams were practicing informal interviews on each other, with Heinrich playing the role of supervisor. When comfortable with the ethnographic guidelines, they'd return to Fort Araby and the Village to carry out their work in a far more systematic fashion, with a far better perspective on what they were doing.

The American was back at his hotel preparing for the next phase of his contribution. It was also the case that his TV was picking up some American football. Football and crime shows were much to his liking: "They keep me off the streets."

Liz had been pulled back from the field to prepare for the experts survey, the Eurogang instrument that would assess the general sweep of the gang problem in the city. André's role in this would not be to carry out the survey; Keller led him into agreement that many respondents might be offended by his role as a police officer. But he had an overview of agencies and officials in Euroburg that might be aware of various kinds of youth groups. He would work with the others to develop the list of experts (broadly defined) for the survey, including a review of Magda's compilation of seven studies that have used expert surveys. Magda would supervise the enterprise, all the way from overseeing the list, to encouraging people to respond, to guiding Liz in the survey process. The data analysis would be in Liz's hands.

Magda had been getting closer to Liz over the past few weeks, concerned that Liz had effectively been closed out of the direct field work in the Middle East neighborhoods and also aware that Liz continued to be concerned about Heinrich's safety. Heinrich had become Liz's world, the project merely the setting for it.

Magda was a wonderful combination of obsessive thoroughness and attention to detail on professional matters – perfect for a staff supervisor – and nurturing supporter and standard setter for younger students and team members. She remembered their birthdays with lunches and token gifts. In the project, her interest was more in process than substance – she was certainly new to gangs – but a quick study in any case. The support she supplied for the staff members compensated for Keller's stiffer, more impersonal style. He is, after all, *The Professor*, but he fully realizes what she does for him. Further, he is grateful, even relieved, that her loyalty is less to him as a person than to the tasks they take on at the institute.

For the experts survey, perhaps the most important of the project instruments for political purposes, Keller will set the table but turn routines over to Magda with full confidence that they will get a good reading on the street gangs of Euroburg. He led the meeting off by pointing out that, with the exception of the police in some cities, no one person or agency was likely to have a comprehensive overview of street gangs – how many, of what sort, where, and so on. Thus the Eurogang experts survey was designed to capture many views and it was up to the researchers to "make sense" of the various reports. To this end, it was necessary to put together a rather thorough list of respondents ("experts," he noted, was perhaps too flattering a term under the circumstances).

The survey instructions, he pointed out as he gave copies to Magda, André, and Liz permit data collection via mail, or phone interview or personal interview or email. His own preference is the phone or personal interview, but Magda can decide with André and Liz which approach best fits various categories of respondents. He, himself, never would use e-mail. Together, they then consider likely kinds of "experts":

School officials and security personnel

Youth agency directors, public and private

Neighborhood Centers

Church officials and youth counselors

Local representatives of the state ministries of welfare, immigration, justice

Police, court, and correctional officials assigned to minors and young adults

Directors and security personnel in the housing developments

Recreation personnel – officials, coaches, parent group chairs

Street corner workers

Neighborhood leaders of various sorts

Merchant's Association (modern versions of the old guilds)

This preliminary list would grow and be refined, Keller pointed out, with confirmation of names, addresses, phone numbers, and the like. He then reviewed the survey form itself with the group. The first page contained instructions for the researchers, not the respondents. The second page had the instructions for the respondents, including emphasis on the Eurogang definition of street gangs. This page established the respondents' knowledge of current or former gangs. The third page obtained descriptive data on each gang known to the respondent. It included the items operationalizing the definition components and other common descriptors as well as a lead into the five "scenarios" on the following page that described the gang structure in the Maxson/Klein typology. The last page sought information about the respondent and his knowledge of other possible respondents and gang programs.

The survey form, Keller pointed out, was relatively brief and straightforward so that even busy bureaucrats could fill it out in a minimum of time. One of its main functions, of course, was to get a grip on the extent of a city's gang program. Another, critical to the multi-method approach, was in the definitional items and gang-type scenarios since these data could then be directly compared to data collected in the ethnographies and youth surveys. The items sought identical information.

Magda would meet soon with André and Liz to go over the survey form item by item, instruction by instruction, and discuss any problems they might foresee. Magda would establish procedures for preliminary review of answers received and for modifying the respondent list. But compared to the tasks of the ethnographers, they agreed, they were getting the easiest piece of the gang puzzle. André could fit in nicely, Liz could find a research process fully her own, and Magda could supervise easily while taking a responsibility for the next, far more complex operation, the youth survey.

22. The Youth Survey

With both the Middle East ethnographies and the experts survey well under way, the weeks passed rapidly and without incident. André's colleagues had made no further headway in their investigation of the Smokes assaulters; no informants had been located. Preliminary responses to the experts survey suggested a surprise, the possible existence of a third street gang. If true, it was located in the backwater canals area, largely overlooked.

Local merchants and several school officials gave superficial descriptions of a group called The Robber Barons. When queried about this, André confessed to never having heard of them. Further inquiries to his juvenile officer colleagues revealed the names of a number of theft and robbery suspects in the area. By and large they had yielded individual arrests with no hint of gang affiliation. The American consultant's parting advice was to look for this group in the responses to the youth survey from schools in the backwater canal district.

The consultant left for home after agreeing to develop a census of gang types reported in European gang literature. This could be done at home just as easily as in Euroburg. He left as well with a large extra bag, filled with Christmas goodies bought during a shopping spree in the company of Keller's wife. He found clothing for family members, craft items for personal friends, and credible souvenirs for office staff. It was getting cold in Europe, and consulting did not require suffering.

Keller's next task was to get the youth survey under way. He knew that Magda had already compiled reports of 15 gang studies in nine countries that had used some form of youth surveys. It would be a complex task and he felt the need to be directly on top of it. Of all the Eurogang Program's research instruments, the youth survey is the most "American" in its derivation. In just twelve typed pages it covers a host of issues narrowed down from prior extensive gang research in the U.S. Most scales and items had proven their utility, with established reliability and validity data. They came from three principal sets of American projects: (a) the "Causes and Correlates" longitudinal studies in Rochester, Denver, and Pittsburgh, (b) Esbensen's longitudinal evaluation of the G.R.E.A.T. gang prevention projects in a score of large and small school systems, and (c) the cross-sectional gang/nongang comparisons of Maxson and Klein in Los Angeles, Long Beach, and San Diego. Many of the items in the Eurogang youth survey had "survived" use in all of these gang projects. Others were added over several years in response to specific concerns of European researchers.

By the time of Keller's decision to rely on the Eurogang instruments, the youth survey had been translated (and back translated) from English into Dutch, French, German, Norwegian, Russian, and Spanish, with others under way. It had been pre-tested in either interview or questionnaire form both in schools and correctional facilities in the U.S., the Netherlands, France, Germany, Norway, and Russia on youths ranging from twelve to eighteen years of age. It was, as Keller told his team, as "ready to go as any instrument I have ever seen in criminological research."

Seven items operationalize the Eurogang definition of street gangs. They are directly comparable to items in the experts survey and the ethnographic guidelines. Twenty-one items in all are considered absolutely core items by the Program. These include items pertinent to establishing the Maxson/Klein gang typology, and can be compared to the typology scenarios in the experts survey.

Other items, highly recommended since the survey generally takes under an hour to administer, include a 20-item self-report delinquency scale, a short victimization scale, a delinquency scale about one's own gang, and an 18-item scale on factors predictive of gang (versus other groups) joining. Additional items include other risk factors and community factors. Researchers can easily add items to these core requirements and suggestions, constrained only by the administration time that seems feasible.

Once this instrument was selected for the Euroburg project, Keller's major remaining decision had to do with sampling. Here, too, the Eurogang

Program made life far simpler through the mechanism of Manchester's STAGE proposal. After heavy consultation with core Eurogang leaders and directors of the nine collaborating national teams, the Manchester team settled on a basic sample of 2000 students of "compulsory school age" in each site, with the questionnaire form of the survey administered in classroom settings. Multi-stage cluster sampling was the chosen approach for schools and an eventual 75 classes within them in each site.

Rather than a city-wide school sample which might yield far too few delinquent group members, the STAGE proposal specified sampling of schools "serving areas of social exclusion" thus improving the chances of capturing gang youth and providing comparability with youth captured in the ethnographies. Special attention would be given to schools designed with programs for socially excluded youth.

Keller and Magda would take on the tasks of liaisons with school officials, working out the timing of the survey (preferably early spring), selection of schools, gaining cooperation of teachers, getting parental permission where necessary, and all other political and administrative necessities. The mayor's office and the Euroburg ministry of education would be engaged first in order to clear as many bureaucratic hurdles as possible. These were not tasks to be assigned to "mere" graduate students.

Still, one issue bothered the team. It was very conceivable that many youngsters in both Fort Araby and the Village would not be found in the public schools, or might be found only in madrasahs, the Muslim religious schools. They would try to obtain household samples or, if need be, snowball samples with the aid of the housing authorities, the state immigration ministry, and their ethnographic field teams. There was no telling how successful this would be, but, as Magda stated the problem, "We can't very well afford to exclude socially excluded youth – that's where so many of our gang members come from. At least we have the advantage of having teams already in there." And Keller added another caveat; if the expert reports were correct of a Robber Baron gang in the backwater canals area, they'd have to be sure to sample in those schools as well. They don't, he suggested, contain the same "socially excluded youth" they talk about in the Middle East housing areas.

While the ethnographies and experts survey were going on, it was clear that staffing was not adequate to stay on top of this large school survey. Conrad would be given a central role, but other students would have to be hired for a few months to handle the survey administration in the schools. Keller would contact professors in the University's teacher training programs to get candidates. Conrad and Magda would see to their training and coordination in the field. "Bad things happen in large school surveys," Keller told them;

"We'll have to be very alert to reports of problems, and very sensitive to the concerns of teachers and school administrators. This school world is a world of bureaucracies and minor politicians with turfs to protect."

Fortunately, the progress of the experts survey was such that Liz would soon have some freed-up time on the project. She would be next in line to help with further forms of data collection. The overall project was large and complex, but Keller was pleased with the caliber of his team members. He had "lucked out," he told the deputy mayor when they came together for lunch before the Christmas break.

23. Crossing Borders: Gang Types and Ethnicities

To: Prof. Martin Keller @fue.edu

Dear Martin;

I'm sending this by e-mail but also faxing a copy in case Magda is not there to serve your immediate needs. It is the report I promised you, summarizing the European gang literature on gang types and origins of the members. Most of this material results from our own Eurogang Program and some of my own visits, so I don't claim it to be altogether thorough.

In addition, what I have for you as context for thinking of your own Euroburg gangs is complicated by the nature of the available reports:

1. Some of the reports were written before or during the time of the gang typology's development. Thus description of types, or placement on the variables comprising the types, are sometimes missing.

2. A few of the reports reflect the ambivalence of the author about the relevance of the typology to the European situation.

3. Gangs change, sometimes changing from one type to another. Only rarely do we have reports noting such changes (Kazan and Oslo being exceptions).

4. Some countries do not permit official collection of ethnic or national origin of their immigrant gang populations. One, for instance, reports on Muslim gangs without mentioning whether they are Moroccan, or Turkish, or Algerian, or whatever.

5. And, of course, we simply don't have gang reports from some countries and from many cities within the others. A full gang census might substantially alter what I report here.

Still, a few generalizations do emerge. I am particularly interested in them because of the contrast they present to well established American patterns. In the U.S., for instance, the predominant gang form is the compressed gang, although the sample survey from The National Youth Gang Center (unpublished) suggested a surprisingly large number of traditional gangs. Ethnic and racial gangs predominate here – African American and Hispanic – with some controversy about the number of white gangs. These latter tend to be found more often in smaller cities and rural areas where research on gangs is less common and police reports are less reliable. We also have larger but scattered pockets of Asian gangs (Chinese, Japanese, Korean, Cambodian, Vietnamese) and a few Pacific Islander (Filipino, Tongan, Samoan). Still, the overall picture is of black and Hispanic gangs (or Latino, depend on which part of the country one is from).

What I can offer you now is a summary of reports from Sweden, Denmark, Norway, Finland, Germany, France, Spain, Italy, Belgium, the Netherlands, England (and Scotland), and Russia. As to the five kinds of gangs in the Maxson/Klein typology, I have yet to see a description of a collective gang, the sort of amorphous neighborhood aggregation described by Fleisher in Kansas City, for example. Very few traditional gangs are reported – Berlin, Kazan, and most recently Oslo (but Patrick's 1970s book on Glasgow gangs certainly fits here). Only in Manchester have I seen a Neo-traditional gang described. Traditional and Neo-traditional gangs, because of their continuing self-regeneration, take many years to form, so their relative absence in Europe so far is not surprising. But, Martin, you may be growing one in Euroburg – the Smokes.

We are left then, with the compressed gang form (primarily adolescent, not large, not normally around for more than five or a few more years), and the specialty gangs, those smaller groups that concentrate on a very few primary forms of illegality. I have found descriptions of compressed gangs in England, Denmark, Germany, the Netherlands, Norway, and Sweden. Specialty gangs seem the most common, particularly because young skinhead groups often fall under this category. Skins have been reported in Russia, England, Denmark, Sweden, Germany, Norway, and Belgium. Other specialty gangs have been noted in the Netherlands and Germany. I wonder if your Robber Barons that you mentioned to me will be comparable to these.

As to ethnicity or nationality, Europe shows a far more varied pattern than the U.S. England and Norway seem to reflect this in particular. All the countries with specialty gangs other than the Netherlands and Germany have indigenous (i.e. non-immigrant, non-refugee) gangs – skinheads. But beyond them, the number of immigrant gang types is striking: Tatar, Afro-Caribbean, Pakistani, Indian, Chinese, Antillean, Surinamese, Moroccan, Turkish, Algerian, Ausseidler, Sicilian and Calabrian, Somali, Iranian, Finnish, Vietnamese, Filipino, Ecuadorian, Colombian (but no North Americans, tell Heinrich). Wherever the immigration and refugee flows yield sufficient numbers of marginalized populations, Europe seems to add them to its own count of indigenous gangs. It's not a pretty pattern, but it's also not a surprising pattern. My principal concern for you folks is that this may go on long enough to spawn Neo-traditional and traditional gangs. Once you have them, you may never see the end of them. Let's therefore pay special attention to Fort Araby and the Smokes.

On a far lighter note, please tell your charming spouse that before leaving you for Christmas I returned to a Moroccan shop we wandered through. As a result, my wife will receive as a present a hammered brass platter with beautifully intricate, etched eastern patterns of varying hues. I don't know how they make these, but I feel as though we've acquired a museum piece. When your wife opens her shop, let me know: we'll visit and buy.

24. City Descriptors Survey

At the very first Eurogang Program workshop, there was discussion about establishing the community contexts of street gangs. Prof. Hans-Jurgen Kerner pushed hard on the necessity of selecting social and demographic descriptors of gang-involved cities, and his colleague Elmar Weitekamp took up the challenge as leader of a city descriptor working group. It was recognized early that no one person, nor even a large working group, could determine what information was uniformly or even widely available across scores of cities in a dozen or more countries. What was needed, then, was a way to allow gang researchers to *consider* what information they could count on for each city. The result is the City Descriptor Survey, an instrument not for assessing actual data but for assessing first what data might be available.

This was the fourth Eurogang Program instrument to be developed, and in truth perhaps the least used to date. It is a complex instrument and requires researchers to delve into areas with which many are not very familiar – city, regional, and national data sources. Let's take the easiest case for the Euroburg team: in terms of population size, how does their city compare with other gang-involved cities (or non-gang-involved cities, if we can be sure which these are)? The team came up with these preliminary lists of gang cities from readily available public documentation:

Similar Size	Larger	Smaller
Antwerp	Amsterdam	Bergen
Bremen	Berlin	Gothenberg
Copenhagen	Birmingham	Lausaune
Frankfurt	Brussels	Sarajevo
The Hague	Kazan	Tubingen
Helsinki	London	
Liverpool	Moscow	
Manchester	Paris	
Oslo		
Rotterdam		
Stockholm		
Stuttgart		
Toulouse		

Would that all city descriptors were so readily available! But they are not, and the team would have to spend time on unfamiliar grounds to assess data availability. Fortunately, faculty and students elsewhere in the Free University could be helpful – sociologists, demographers, city planners, education programs, economists, historians, and political scientists, along with colleagues in the criminology institute. This was a good time to get on with the task. Winter had fully arrived. The tourists were gone, the youth survey was being introduced to school officials, the gang members in the Middle East were hunkering down in their housing developments. The backwater canals were freezing over so that ice skaters could show their skills (and fall through the weak areas where alert citizens used ropes and floats to pull them out). Euroburg, like many other continental cities, faced the colder winters by turning inward. The homeless suffered in shelters and abandoned buildings, the crime-prime youth lived off their earlier spoils, and only the hospitals maintained a decent level of activity. All in all, a good opportunity to consider city descriptors.

There are two basic reasons to do so. First some of these descriptors, alone and in combination, may serve as "risk variables" or predictors of gang presence and activity. Second, they may help to place the city in the broader context of urban life and problems, showing what is shared (and inevitable?) and what is unique (and remediable?). Population size is the easiest example; from there on, it gets tougher. For example, how many European cities have adequate data on the size, nature, density, and segregation of their various immigrant and refugee populations? How many cities are aware of current changes in the nature of these populations?

The city descriptors survey is a four page matrix of potential data. It asks only (but "only" is quite misleading) five basic questions about a series of descriptors in eight broad areas. Technically, therefore, it seeks to know if data are available in 40 (5 times 8) categories. The five basic questions for each area are these:

A. Do you have *Access* (not collected, difficult to obtain; readily available);

B. *Availability* (not collected, yearly, other period of time);

C. *Cost* of collection

D. *Comparability* of data across cities in your country;

E. *Available at Neighborhood Level*

These five questions at the top of each page of the survey form are then applied to the eight broad areas down the left hand side, to form the matrix. The eight areas are these:

1. *Demographic* (age, sex, race of population; age, sex, and race for youth; household divorce rate and children per family; migration).

2. *Economic* (employment sectors, levels, locations, income; unemployment rate; employment opportunities, especially for youth).

3. *Education* (type and number of institutions, literacy rates, school completion rates, school access, public vs. private auspices, compulsory school age, accessibility of schools).

4. *Socio-Structural* (social cohesion and social capital as in neighborhood bonding, sense of community, and organizational involvement; social segregation).

5. *Social Context* (languages, historical events, important cultural characteristics, social inequality, citizen surveys).

6. *Political/Administrative* (electoral as in voting behavior, voting turnout; local government as in party structure, policies on crime, juvenile crime, and youth welfare; nongovernment organizations, the number and sources of support; police; youth programs, including numbers and types, geographic accessibility and transportation available).

7. *Crime/Deviance* (in general; recorded offenses on juvenile crime, gang crime, age-specific homicide rate, drug-related deaths, public disorder crimes, unintentional/accidental deaths, victimization data, fear of crime data).

8. *Physical Characteristics* (land use, transportation – including modes of youth transportation and legal driving age - housing density, building period and type, physical disorder, concentration of youth entertainment, ability of youth to communicate across distance).

Now, clearly, not all of these items will be available and accessible in each gang city. In a number of instances, definitional problems appear to be considerable. More prior use of the city descriptors survey might well have improved the situation. Nonetheless, the survey portrays a vast array of potentially relevant data, and it would behoove any research team to analyze data accessibility for its project. And that is the purpose of the form, to initiate the study of the possibilities, to understand what is available and what might be sought.

Keller and his team had much work to do on city descriptors, starting first with a discussion of which variables were most relevant to the Euroburg project. The process would go on for many months, fortunately not affecting the other research procedures. But for purposes of final reports and of integrating Euroburg gang data with those from other cities, the process would need to move ahead. It would not be the research team's favorite expenditure of time.

25. Prevention and Intervention Survey

The experts' survey asks for the respondents' knowledge of gang programs in the city. The prevention and intervention survey, the fifth of the Eurogang Program instruments, is designed to follow up on the best of those programs or any others known to exist.

In the United States, of course, there is a long tradition of gang prevention and intervention programs, because there is a long tradition of street gangs. There is also a long tradition of programs with no demonstration of success, accompanied by a long tradition of only anecdotal reports of success, of conventional wisdoms about success, and of unsupported agency and political claims of success. One might fairly ask: If there has been so much "success," how is it that street gangs in the U.S. keep growing and proliferating throughout the country?

One of the earliest rationales for undertaking the Eurogang Program was that in Europe, because its street gang problem was relatively new and not yet institutionalized, perhaps the gang problem could be contained before it got out of the control of citizens and officials. The failure of gang programming in the U.S. need not predict to such failure elsewhere.

By "prevention" was meant developing procedures to head off gang formation and gang-joining by new members. By intervention was meant procedures to weed out or wean away youth already involved in gang life. Neither of these terms was meant to include anti-gang police or court suppression programs, such as Andre Mellers' gang work in Euroburg, although certainly suppression approaches should coordinate with prevention and intervention services.

In Euroburg, preliminary data from the experts' survey yielded only one known instance of a gang program. Several respondents listed the police, improperly, including two police officials. One respondent mentioned general school recreation programs, and two church officials nominated their own youth programs, but without any indication of how they related to gang problems. Neither church was located anywhere near The Middle East (and two mosque leaders chose not to respond to the survey). The university's gang project was mentioned by these public officials as a gang intervention project, bringing smiles to most team members' faces. Keller said, "I hope my criminology colleagues don't hear that I'm collecting data to reduce gang activity. We're researchers, not social workers." This time it was Sgt. Mellers' turn to smile, almost snicker.

One program was listed by a school security officer and a housing administrator in The Village. The name of the program was Alexander Aziz. The administrator knew that Alexander had been assigned by the state ministry, not by any local entity. That was it; in Euroburg, gang prevention and intervention were represented according to community experts by one third-generation Russian Arab. There was room for improvement.

Of course, that raised the question of whether or not to go ahead with the final Eurogang survey. A quick phone call to the American consultant at his home revealed that he had had similar low responses during his visits to gang cities in Scandinavia and the continent, but that he had nonetheless been able to "sniff out" as he put it several interesting intervention projects – one in Berlin, one in Stuttgart, one in Stockholm, one in Barcelona, and a relevant "bullying intervention" in Norway. He had also been told of several candidates in England. He urged carrying on with the survey.

The question for the team remained, who should they survey about gang programs that don't seem to exist. The answer came once one reviewed the survey form. The Eurogang working group had anticipated the problem, and had decided it would not seek answers from agency or program officials. It was much influenced by the American experience of failures in program design, program implementation, and program evaluation. The prevention and intervention survey was designed to be filled out by researchers, by criminologists. "Oh my God," said Liz to everyone's amusement. "We're supposed to survey ourselves!" Martin Keller did not share in the amusement. He had known, of course, what was coming, and now he reviewed the form for his team – the piñata had been broken open.

The intention of the form is clear from the beginning; it asks for the name of the program administrator, the name and contact for the researcher, and "a full description of research that provided a foundation for the intervention including research reports, publications, etc." It is clear, then, that The Eurogang Program intended to learn only about "evidence-based" programs, thus excluding almost all gang programs in existence. This is an extremely narrow focus, Keller acknowledged to his team, but it reflects the frustrations that American program evaluators and scholars have experienced over several decades. "And," he added, "it puts the horse before the cart for a change, showing interest in programs that people like us – research scholars – should attempt to initiate."

The full group then reviewed the three-page survey form. It sets any target gang program within a context of other targets – delinquency generally, other youth groups, and so on. It also establishes the program context in the several areas of prevention, intervention, and suppression. It asks about program connections to criminal justice, social welfare, and immigration. Finally, it seeks information about program evaluation.

In some sense, the research team seemed relieved; it was clear that the survey would not apply in Euroburg – not yet, in any case. Even Alexander's efforts did not fit. On the other hand, it meant that assessing the city's response to the gang problem would be assessed only by the minimal information from the experts' survey. They might want, therefore, to follow up on the answers from some of those respondents. The whole situation gave Keller an opportunity to stress once more for his team the importance of what they were doing – gathering truly basic local information, and positioning themselves to fit under a much larger and highly relevant umbrella, the Eurogang Program. (And, he would remind himself, it was he who set things up this way; he was pleased with himself).

The Euroburg project was back to its first four Eurogang Program instruments, not five. Further, the city descriptors survey was designed for context-setting, for sociological analysis. In addition the experts' survey was designed mostly to indicate how broad the gang problem might be. By now, the team members thought they knew the answer to this. Thus, for most of the team, the project was devolving into a two-instrument project, the ethnographies and the youth survey. But they would not acknowledge this publicly, that is, not to the professor nor to Magda.

26. Ethnographic Reports: Smokes and Zealots

By early spring, things were moving along. The experts' survey had been completed, and the data were being prepared by Liz. The youth survey had been initiated in the first sets of schools and procedural modifications were being implemented to gain easier entrée to the next set. Conrad had been put in touch with Martin Keller's faculty colleagues about determining what city descriptors might be available, and how to access them. The two field teams in the Middle East were orienting themselves to the requirements of the ethnographic guidelines.

Keller was aware that these ethnographies held the most interest for public officials as well as for many of his Eurogang Program colleagues. The American consultant had been e-mailing requests for some additional data about the two gangs to see how they compared to European gangs already described in the program literature. Keller called a special meeting of the field teams, but when they gathered, he was not there. Magda explained that he was lecturing in Copenhagen where new gang problems were rumored. She would conduct the ethnography meeting.

Those present were Heinrich and Dirk for the Smokes, Alexander for the Zealots, and Liz who would eventually be in charge of coding their field notes and interviews. She needed to hear their reports to help her develop categories for the coding scheme. Magda's instructions were simple: "The professor wants your preliminary findings for direct comparison of the two gangs. You've been talking with each other along the way, so it should be pretty easy. You have in front of you the last two pages of the guidelines. We're going to go through the list of thirteen questions that will comprise your face sheet at the end of the research. What you report now can, and probably will change by then, so don't get fixed on these first results. This session is meant to be preliminary, suggestive, and will inform Liz for her coding process and the professor for his conversations with his colleagues. Are we clear? Is this okay?"

Everyone nodded and looked at the thirteen questions. Heinrich and Dirk pulled out piles of field notes. Alexander did not. "All right, I'll pose the questions in order. Hein, or Dirk, you answer first for the Smokes, then Alexander for the Zealots. Ready?"

"Number one: average age and age range for the members."

Heinrich: "I'd guess the average Smoke at about 17 or 18. I've got real young ones coming in at 11 and 12. The oldest – somewhere around the mid-twenties, I guess – the elders."

Dirk: "Actually, the guys that started the Smokes after they were attacked 15 years ago by a few skinheads must be closer to 30 now, but I don't know that you could call them active. It's all in the head; one older guy says he just keeps an eye out for the group but a couple of others told me, 'Once you're a Smoke, you're always a Smoke.' I'll bet Sgt. Mellers would count them as Smokes still."

Alexander: "It's different with the Zealots. Remember many of them are eastern refugees, the Balkans and Iraq and Afghanistan. They're first generation youth, mostly adolescents. I'd say 13 to 18, average around 16. They don't hang around as long after school age; they have to find jobs or move on."

"Ok, I think I know the answer to number two, gender composition," said Magda.

Heinrich: "Almost totally male. A few girls try to hang with them, but they're shunned and told to stay home where they belong."

Alexander: "Same thing, but there are fewer young women as refugees in any case."

Liz: "You know, it's real hard to be a good feminist in this world of theirs."

Alexander: "Yes, and that doesn't bother me at all."

"Number three; ethnicity – I mean, beyond simply Muslim."

Heinrich: "Principally Moroccan, and then Turks. They were the first brought in as guest workers, and some families have stayed into a third generation. There are sprinklings of others in the buildings, but most don't get into the gang; Bosnians, former Soviet republic people like 'Samurai', the scariest of the bunch."

Alexander: "As I said, there are some 'leftover' Turkish guest worker families in The Village, but it's a newer facility so it has more recent arrivals. Even among them, the ones who join the Turks in the Zealots are the most recent refugees escaping really nasty, war-torn areas like Bosnia, Kosovo, Iraq, and Afghanistan. A few Chechens also. It's really that war escape that binds them, even more than religion. That, and the disrespect they get from the older immigrant groups, including the Smokes."

"Ok; number four is immigrant status, and we've just included that. So, number five, is illegal behavior accepted and performed?"

"Yes," from all three reporters.

"Ok; number six, what are the most common crimes?"

Heinrich: "Despite what the cops report, the most common ones are the non-serious ones: drug use, graffiti and vandalism, thefts of various kinds, threats to do this or that to people downtown. There's fighting, but usually without weapons and certainly without guns."

Dirk: "you could add underage drinking among some of them, despite the religious taboos against it. Some selling of hashish also."

Alexander: "It's pretty much the same for the Zealots, although we don't see the drinking and we do see or at least we hear about carrying weapons of all sorts as defensive behavior."

Magda: "Then you're convinced, so far, that the news and police reports about violent crime are exaggerated?"

Heinrich: "They're way off base for the Smokes, that's for sure."

Alexander: "And the Zealots, too. I think Sgt. Mellers realizes this now, because we've been talking about it. But you folks need to get to that reporter of yours and hush him up."

Magda: "Thank you – we're trying. Number seven is alcohol and drug use, and I guess you've answered that already. So, number eight, group size."

Heinrich: "I think the original estimates hold up pretty well, depending on how you count, especially the youngest and the oldest. If you include the young 12 and 13 year olds sort of trying on gang status and the elders who are not very active, if at all, you could list maybe 125 Smokes. Otherwise, you could claim closer to eighty or ninety."

Dirk: "I like to keep count of guys who are active or visible on the streets or hanging around the common rooms and areas in Fort Araby. I don't think there's more than 50 or 60 of them really active."

Alexander: "The Zealots are clearly a smaller group. Even adding actives and fringe members, I'd say fifty or fewer at this point. And of course there's never more than a dozen actually, physically together at the same time except when a special meeting is called."

Magda: "Special meeting? What's that all about? Who calls it?"

Alexander: "Well, a couple of times older guys have gathered the troops to talk about responding to threats or incursions by the Smokes. And I've held formal meetings three times now to get my messages across – you can talk more efficiently to 30 guys at once than you can to 30 guys individually."

Dirk: "Oh boy – you could be building up gang cohesiveness that way, bringing them together, legitimizing them. That scares me."

Alexander: "They're already cohesive. That's one of the things we talk about."

Magda: "Ok, let's save that discussion for when the professor is here. Number nine is about gang names: Smokes and Zealots, right?"

Heinrich: "Well, a few of my elders still call themselves "Duskies," the original label pinned on them. Then we've got Senior Smokes, Junior Smokes, and West and North Smokes based on which building they're from in Fort Araby."

Dirk: "And I just came across a clique of eleven and twelve year olds from the East building that claim they are 'The New Smokes.' I hope no one encourages them."

Alexander: "Nope; all we've got is Zealots, all the same breed."

"Okay, number ten: how about spending time in public places?"

Heinrich: "Whenever possible. The Fort is crowded, constantly under the eye of fathers and grandfathers with no tolerance for kids hanging around aimlessly. So Smokes are outside, riding the subway, downtown in the shopping areas and arcades and Old Town, and in Grand Park."

Dirk: "And don't forget the Akbar Café."

Alexander: "Same pattern for the Zealots, except they can hang in The Village a lot, around the market area and around the two mosques as well."

"Number eleven is subgroups. Heinrich and Dirk have already answered this for the Smokes. What about Zealot cliques."

Alexander: "It's different. There are no named cliques. I mean, sure friends hang out together, they group up some on the basis of residence sections of The Village, classes in school, and family relations – brothers and cousins sort of thing. But this is all very informal. They all think of themselves as one big clique, if you will, and don't mix much with the other youth groups around The Village. They're all just Zealots; their world is Zealots and non-Zealots."

"Ok, number twelve, what term do they use to define themselves?"

Dirk: "I've asked Smokes if they think of themselves as a gang, and they say 'Yes, sure,' and sometimes they'll even refer to famous gangs like Crips and Bloods. For them, there's pride in being a gang."

Alexander: "I don't like the word gang, I think it's stigmatizing, so I've never asked them the question like Dirk. But they know they're different, so they'd probably accept the word readily enough."

"Ok; finally, are they territorial?"

Heinrich: "Not like American gangs. The Smokes know that Fort Araby is theirs, but no one even challenges them there. They don't need to defend it, but surely they would if they had to. They're very suspicious of outsiders like me and Dirk, anyone new, anyone non-Muslim. If they have a territory, you might say it's downtown areas where they hang, but I don't see them fighting for those areas. So, they're territorial in the sense that they claim Fort Araby, but not in the sense that they feel the need to defend it."

Dirk: "It's important to recognize, though, that they haven't really been challenged. I think guys like Muhammed and Samurai would require their cliques to be very combative if someone like the Zealots or some skinheads were to try to put them down, or 'invade' The Fort in some sense."

Alexander: "I don't sense that kind of territoriality in the Zealots. It's not so much space that holds them together as back home rivalries and tribal wars. And also, remember that most of them struggle with language here; they mostly speak native or Arabic languages. Smokes call them 'foreigners.' That's just asking for trouble. Some of them are more like vigilante warriors than gang-bangers. We think of them more as victims, not as aggressors, but victims ready to fight back."

Magda: "Well, those are indeed very interesting differences. I'm very proud of you all for your insights about these young people. These descriptions will surely be of interest to the professor and his Eurogang colleagues. But let me ask you to expand on a few more things. I'll keep recording your comments for the record, but I want Liz to be able to think about these other issues as well. For instance, the professor puts a lot of emphasis on the cohesiveness of street gangs. How do you see this in your groups?"

Heinrich: "I don't – at least, I don't see anything remarkable. You've got a hundred or more people aged 12 to maybe 30. How can they be tight with each other? I mean, yeah there's a lot of rhetoric about watching each others' backs, about 'us versus them,' and so on, but you never see really big groups in one place at the same time. So if a street gang is supposed to be really cohesive, then maybe the Smokes don't measure up well to being a street gang – just a large assemblage of unhappy and alienated outsiders."

Dirk: "Actually, I think Hein is answering for the forest, not the trees. If you look instead at the cliques, observe who hangs with whom, and if you listen to the talk, the cohesiveness is there, but it's in the cliques. It's in the separate age groups and in the West and North buildings. The cliques are fairly cohesive subgroups with a bunch of less connected members around them. Lots of guys don't fit in the cliques, so that gives the appearance of non-cohesion. I think you have to see both patterns, tighter groups and looser overall affiliations. Ok, Hein?"

Heinrich: "Yeah, that's good. Dirk and I tend to look at different things, I guess, even though he doesn't leave me alone out there. He's my male mother these days!"

Alexander: "The Zealots aren't like that. They're a smaller outfit, closer in age, and with a higher proportion of victimized refugees as I told you earlier. They are a pretty cohesive, single group even though there are smaller little networks of family and friend connections. For the Zealots, the one-for-all-and-all-for-one rhetoric is pretty real. It's a different kind of gang."

Liz: "Boy, they really are, aren't they. You know, if you go back to that gang typology the American keeps talking about, it really fits here. The Zealots are a 'compressed gang'; the Smokes sound very much like a 'traditional' or 'neo-traditional' gang – probably becoming 'traditional' in any case. It makes the typology come alive; street observation meets theory!"

Magda: "Thank you. You're a sharp bunch of people. Here's another question, especially for Hein and Dirk: given all these cliques, are there clique leaders, youth who 'call the shots' for others?"

Heinrich: "Sure, but there's a lot of variation. This kid Mustafa, my special informant, knows a lot, but he's really a 'wannabe,' a kid desperate to be accepted. He got badly beaten by Samurai for trying too hard, got told to go home and grow up. Samurai is a strong leader, but he's seen as a little weird and unpredictable. It's just that no one dares challenge him. Incidentally, I finally learned his real name: Sarkand Kazakh. Mohammed gets a lot of respect from the Seniors; so does Kemal from the next group. Then guys like Aziz and Khalid are popular with the younger guys, but they deny they are leaders. And then there's ---"

Alexander: "Whoa! Wait a minute. Magda, I'm sorry, but I don't think we should be doing this, naming names like this. Our work with the Zealots is based in part on our respecting confidentiality, respecting their privacy. Maybe for research purposes you have a reason for names, but our joining this team doesn't mean we give up our principles as advocates and service providers for our young people. I'm not going to use their names, even around this table. I'm sorry, but that's firm."

Heinrich: "Aw, shit man, it's just between us."

Alexander: "But I can't know that. You got a reporter – this van der Waal guy – nosing around. You write reports; you visit other cities; you give reports to the deputy major; worst of all, you share information with Sgt. Mellers. You call it data; he calls it criminal intelligence. We just can't be a part of it."

Magda: "Ok, Alexander's position is a legitimate concern, and we won't resolve it here. I withdraw the question. We may have to ask Prof. Keller to lead a discussion about the handling of personal identities. Lots of gang researchers and gang workers have had to deal with the issue, so I'm sure we'll find some useful guidelines. Until then, I recommend that we avoid naming names, and guard our field notes very carefully.

"I think that's enough for today in any case. Prof. Keller will be back next week, and he wants to see then if we can wrap up what we've learned from the experts' survey. Progress, progress; what fun!"

27. The Four Gangs of the Experts Survey

To: <u>cmaxson@uci.edu</u>

Remember that old childhood rhyme, "Spring has sprung, the grass has riz, I wonder where the daisies is?" Well, the weather has warmed enough that I'm back in Euroburg. I'm reporting to you because, spring has sprung, the data has riz, and now we know where the gangs is!

I attended a staff meeting of Martin's research team this morning at which his student Liz reported preliminary results from the experts' survey. Because of your work as chair of the Eurogang working group on the experts' survey, and because of our shared interest in how the gang typology works out over here, you are hereby anointed data-audience number one. Briefly, the survey works, and it has produced a picture of four street gangs here. An interesting sidelight (one of two I'll share with you) is that the police gang unit had compiled folders on six local gangs. Three of these are confirmed by the survey data, but three it turns out don't fit the definition of *any durable, street-oriented youth group whose involvement in illegal activity is part of its group identity*. There are the two immigrants/refugee gangs I described to you earlier, and a skinhead gang broadly hinted at earlier and included in the police files although the cops think of them more as a political collective than a gang. But the other three groups labeled street gangs by the gang unit don't fit: one is a small, non-delinquent tagger crew, one is a no-longer existent skinhead group from 20 years ago, and the other is a bunch of wild-haired punkers who do nothing but lounge around public areas with the music turned up to a rebellious volume.

But in addition, there's a specialty gang we had heard of slightly, called The Robber Barons, who concentrate on burglaries and petty thefts. As individuals, these kids were known to the juvenile officers because of their arrest records, but no one had connected them. Thus the gang unit has been unaware of them. It was some businessmen and neighborhood leaders who reported them as a group in the survey responses; that is, it's a victim-nominated gang, rather than a police labeled gang. Interesting twist, no?

The second interesting sidelight comes from a staff meeting a couple of months ago. It took place when the first results were coming in and I was back home. Those early results pretty much confirmed the Skinhead group whose graffiti I had observed earlier, O.T.S. standing for Old Town Skins. Martin declared they needed to get someone into the field to start some ethnographic work on O.T.S., at which point his Swedish student Conrad Eriksson came out of his secret closet.

I had noted earlier that Conrad seemed an ill fit in the Euroburg setting, but also that something else bothered me about him, his tattoo removal scars on neck and arms – very unusual for a young Swede. His secret is that those had been skinhead tattoos, removed when he got exposed to a Swedish anti-skinhead treatment program in Stockholm. I knew about this program, associated with Fryshuset people in Stockholm who also ran a gang outreach program (Mothers and Fathers on the Town) along with other deviance services. Fryshuset turned angry skinhead Conrad into an equally militant anti-skin, labeled Skinheads Against Racism. I've heard of such groups, but not run across them directly.

The upshot of all this is that Conrad "came out" to the research team and volunteered to do the field work on your survey's newly confirmed Skinhead gang. Conrad obviously had a lot of the experience needed to connect with O.T.S., so he got a buzz cut and mildly appropriate clothing (no jack boots!). He headed out and made quick and seemingly successful contacts. He was at the staff meeting this morning, and some of the information reported below comes from him. He's been transformed on the research team from stereotypically quiet Swede to fully participating researcher. Well, whatever it takes!

Now, on to the data reported by Liz. I'll give you the respondent information, and then the summary of the four-gang data that came from the survey. A total of 58 expert respondents have provided data – most by questionnaire or e-mail, some by follow-up phone calls with Magda or Liz, and several by personal interviews by Liz. The breakdown is as follows:

School officials	10
School security	6
Youth agencies	7
Church officials	4
Local reps. of state agencies	3
Police, courts, and corrections	5
Recreation	6
Merchants' Assn.	3
Neighborhood leaders and businessmen	14
Housing directors and security	0

That last figure represents the difficulties of "penetrating" the Muslim projects on the outskirts of town. The plan is to get the street workers there to engage those correspondents, although the team already knows enough about the gangs there to make such an effort more gravy than meat. Overall, the 58 respondents constitute 73% of the 80 on the survey list. This seems pretty good to me, and any success from the street workers would yield an even better showing.

The other significant overall finding has to do with variance of reports over the four revealed street gangs. Decent information on the two immigrant gangs was provided by half of the respondents. The Skinheads (O.T.S.) were described to varying degrees by 25 respondents, but the other specialty gang, The Robber Barons (T.R.B) was described by only 15 people – mostly in the neighborhood and school security categories. The justice officials, including police who had arrested members of the group, had not caught on to their gang status as I noted earlier. Hooray for multi-method research!

Finally, there's this anomaly. Several respondents – inevitably older men who had been active for many years – nominated a skinhead gang that was not O.T.S. Follow-up phone interviews by Magda, with Conrad listening in, revealed this group to go back about 20 years ago – the same gang reported by the gang unit – but to be unconnected to the currently active O.T.S. members. It was this earlier skins gang that had harassed the kids in Fort Araby and led directly to the formation of the Smokes as a defensive gang to begin with. This absolutely mirrors the picture Margy and I received about the origin of the 36-ers gang in Berlin in the early 1990s, a group that eventually became Berlin's first traditional street gang. Wanna form a gang? Turn on the skinheads!

Ok; from the data reported in this morning's meeting by Liz, from notes provided by Magda and from some discussions from the students and field workers, I've put together for you a tabular summary of what has emerged so far about the four street gangs of Euroburg. They seem to fit nicely into the Maxson/Klein typology: the Smokes are a neo-traditional gang, the Zealots a compressed gang, and T.R.B. and O.T.S. are specialty gangs. Here's my table:

	Smokes	Zealots	T.R.B.	O.T.S.
# Members	100+	50-75	15?	25?
Age Range	11-30	13-19	13-16	13-21
Duration	15+ years	<10 years	3 years	5 years
Ethnicity	Mixed Muslim	Mixed Muslim	White	White
Cliques	4 or 5	No	No	No
Street time	Yes	Yes	Yes	Yes
Territorial	Yes	Yes	No	No
Territory Defense	No	No	No	No
Illegal behavior	Versatile	Versatile	Property	Assault, etc.
Alcohol use	Low	Low	Low	High
Drug use	Low	Medium	Low	Medium
Rivals	Yes	Yes	No	No
Scenario type	Neo-Trad.	Compressed	Specialty	Specialty

I'm sure that the continuing research, especially the youth interview, will add some data to some of the above. Still, the patterns look pretty stable to me and give a nice picture of what our research process can yield. Kudos go to Martin's research team for being able to get this far in less than a year and being able to take on the Eurogang instrument package so successfully, to date. The youth interview process is now ongoing, and I'll get a better feeling for that fairly soon as response rates go up.

I want to add two points for you before I wrap this up and go down to the bar for my Ouzo. First, research teams should plan on doing a number of expert surveys in person or by phone. I noted above some advantages, but another is the opportunity to hammer home our definition of street gangs. Some of the returned questionnaires labeled some youth groups as gangs incorrectly. People read but paid little attention to the Eurogang definition. Other questions on the survey made this obvious, so Magda and Liz made personal follow-up contacts to get clarification. This needs to be built into the process.

The second point has to do with the skinhead gang, O.T.S. Some respondents, including the cops, saw them more in political terms rather than as a street gang. Church respondents shared the same pattern – the team got terms for O.T.S. such as mob, hooligans, extremists, and in one case "a bunch of psychopaths" without seeing the group aspect that holds these youth together. These aggressive aspects of the skins seem to trump observation of their cohesion. I'm not saying that all skinheads constitute specialty gangs, but the data here certainly puts the Euroburg skins in that category. And more than the other three groups, the respondents assign a violent character to these gangs. So, incidentally, does Conrad, who is in a special position to make this judgment. He has voiced his concern about likely clashes between O.T.S. and the two Muslim groups. I hope he exaggerates.

28. Background Statement: Assessing Street Gang Violence

[Special Comments from the Author]

The assault on Abu (now fully recovered), the threats on Heinrich, and Conrad's warning about the Old Town Skins keep the team alert to the possibility of gang-related violence, even though its level in Euroburg seems low. In the U.S., one of the most damaging events in street gang history was the publication of Lewis Yablonsky's 1963 book The Violent Gang. It wasn't the book that was damaging. Indeed it provided insightful if controversial notions about gangs based on the author's relatively brief exposure to the scene in New York City. It was the title of the book that was damaging. "The Violent Gang" became an accepted concept, repeated ever since in the minds of the public and public officials. Gang equals violence; violence equals gang. No amount of contrary evidence seems to disconnect those two dots, gang and violence.

In that same year, 1963, a conference on gang research was held to which all the nation's active gang researchers were invited. In one session, panelists discussed the level of violence that was attributed to gangs, and agreed substantially that it had been overstated and constituted only a small portion of gang members' behavior. As the session was about to conclude, Yablonsky stood up at the rear of the conference room, The Violent Gang in his hand, and proclaimed, "Now wait a minute; I have an investment in violence!" He said it in good humor and everyone laughed. But he meant it and for years afterward he continued his proclamations about the prevalence of gang violence.

Yablonsky provided the phrase, and voiced his investment. But others, too, have an investment in gang violence, most notably the media, the police, and public officials; gangs are violent and violence is endemic to street gangs, they believe. Well, this is not what criminological research tells us. The violence is there, but it must be placed in context. Acts of gang violence are common but not predominant. It is the rhetoric of violence that is predominant. One hears it, in the field, more than one sees it. Preliminary indicators from Euroburg suggest the same patterns.

But to understand this, we first have to define out terms again. What do we include under the umbrella of violence? If my loving wife throws a frying pan at my head, is that violence? (It would be to me, I assure you). What if she throws a cup of water at me?

The Eurogang Program encounters street gang members from a number of different cultures. They do not define violence in identical terms. The ISRD program had to exclude the carrying of knives by youth as a delinquent offense because Swiss youth so commonly carry Swiss army knives. Silly example, you say? How about "honor killings" in some Mid-East nations, in many instances approved by the families and unpunished by officials?

In most Western countries, police and courts proclaim a fairly common list of criminal offenses as violent offenses. The list includes murder, shots fired at people, assaults using other weapons (including fists and feet), assaults without weapons (threats, intimidation), armed robbery, rape and sexual assault, weapons possession, brandishing of weapons, and arson (in some cases, not all).

But if we can accept this list as comprising most violence, we have yet more definitional problems to consider. For instance, should we define the level of gang violence according to how much is reported to the police, or how much is reported in victim surveys (where the perpetrators' gang status is often unknown), or how much is admitted by gang members in self-report studies? Victim surveys are pretty useless here; police statistics disproportionately include violent over non-violent offenses. Gang member self-reports are expensive to gather and seldom cover more than one or a few selected gangs in any study. In other words, almost any report of the level or nature of gang violence must be carefully scrutinized before being accepted at face value. If only news reporters like Patrick van der Waal could remember this.

The problem is well illustrated in the first major report from The International Self-Report Delinquency project. The ISRD interview instrument included six personal violence items, and six countries reported their prevalence rates based on these. But five countries included under the category of violence offenses against property, such as graffiti, vandalism, and arson. One has to read this report very carefully, paying special attention to the data tables to appreciate the differences. In the countries using the broader, more inclusive category, "violence" was reported to be, on average, roughly twice as common. The difference is definitional, not behavioral.

Here's an American example. Five police departments reported gang arrest data for a one-year period (Klein and Maxson, 2006). They varied in the inclusiveness of offense categories used. The more categories used, the lower was the percentage of violent offenses out of all offenses recorded. The percentage of violent offenses was 11%, 24%, 29%, 50%, and 56%. In the 11% department, where violence levels approached those taken from self-report studies, 18 different offense categories were used. In the department reporting 56% of all offenses being violent, only nine categories were used. This proportion of gang violence exaggerated by police is a function of how many non-violent kinds of offenses they also bother to record. Yablonsky's "violent gang" was probably, in fact, a relatively non-violent gang. But you can't sell a book titled The Non-Serious Delinquent Gang.

Another example is provided by Esbensen and his colleagues in Denver (1993) using the term "street crime" rather than (but roughly equivalent to) violent crime. These authors found self-reported street crimes to be less common than other serious crimes, minor crimes, alcohol use and drug use, in that order. Only drug sales were less common than street crimes. Examples like this abound in the American gang literature. Gang violence exists, and is a serious matter, but is proportionately minor.

Suppose we look at homicides, that worst of all personal crimes. The extreme is to be found in Los Angeles County (which includes the city of Los Angeles). From 1980 to the present, that area has recorded anywhere from 200 to over 800 "gang related" homicides each year. Those are horrendous numbers. Over 800 victims' families and 800 offenders' families have been directly affected in the worst of those years. Yet across the United States of America, 80 per cent of towns and cities with reported gang problems yield no gang homicides in a given year.

In the five police departments mentioned earlier, the year of data collection showed two homicides out of 1320 recorded gang offenses. Gang homicides are not widely distributed, but concentrated in a few areas. Block and Block (1993) reveal in addition that gang homicides are not evenly distributed among gangs. In Chicago, they found that 10 per cent of the gangs, having 51 per cent of all the city's gang members, accounted for 55 per cent of all gang homicides. So gang-related homicides are relatively rare (when compared to other gang violence and especially non-violence), are concentrated in a few cities and in a few gangs within those cities. No wonder we've never lost a gang researcher by homicide!

There is still another complication to all this. The phrase "gang-related" was used here. But what do we mean by this? It turns out that there are at least three different definitions of a "gang-related" crime. The most restrictive of these is found in some special anti-gang legislation. Good examples are found in California, Nevada, and Illinois, where gang-related means that the crime was specifically "...for the benefit of, at the direction by, or in association with any criminal street gang and with the specific intent to promote, further, or assist" gang goals (California penal code section 186.22). Spain is now considering similar legislation. In other words, the crime is intended for the gang's purpose, not the individual member's purposes. In such a situation, additional years of incarceration can be applied to a convicted offender.

The second definition of gang-relatedness also pertains to gang motive, but in this case to the individual offender's motive due to his (or her) gang membership, a motive not attributable to a non-gang individual. Common examples include a crime committed as a gang initiation, or retaliation against a beating by members of a rival gang, or a crime designed to increase one's reputation in the gang. The crime serves the individual's purpose as a gang member.

The most inclusive of the three definitions, accounting for as many as two-thirds of all "gang-related" crimes, is simply that any crime involving a gang member, as either perpetrator or victim, is gang-related. No imputations of individual or gang-related motive is involved, only the presence of a gang member in the offense. As a common example, profits from drug sales by a gang member usually enrich the seller's purse, but do not usually end up in a gang "treasury".

Or consider the assault on Abu by the Smokes. By the gang-member-involved definition, it was a gang-related offense. Only if the Smokes beat up Abu to enhance their own reputations would it be considered a gang-motivated offense. And only if it was designed to send a message that the Smokes as a group were to be respected would it fit the first, narrowest definition of having the intent to further gang goals. Alexander and his colleagues believed this third definition was correct (the message being sent to Heinrich in particular). But most of the tourist muggings, smash-and-grab burglaries, and individual tagging in subway tunnels committed by

The Smokes would be gang-related due to individual members and group relationship motives – matters of individual gain, not due to specific gang enhancement purposes. The difference may seem "merely academic", but in fact relates directly to how much "gang-related" crime is reported for a city like Euroburg. It can affect the fate of a gang member when he is convicted of a gang offense and the length or severity of his court sentence is determined.

For research purposes, does it matter whether crimes are committed by gang members or non-gang youth? You bet it does. Research in the U.S. (Klein 1995) revealed that gang and non-gang violence differs markedly as to the character of the participants <u>and</u> the character of the circumstances in which the violence takes place. Gang-related violence (defined by gang member involvement, our third, most inclusive criteria) was compared to non-gang violence from the same police jurisdictions and for roughly the same age ranges of the offenders. Gang violence involved:

- More participants
- More victims with no prior contact with the offenders
- More gang member victims
- Younger offenders
- Younger victims
- More male participants
- More minority participants

Gang violence also involved:

- More settings in public places
- More automobiles
- More firearms than other weapons
- A larger number of weapons
- More associated offenses charged
- More unidentified assailants
- More fear of retaliation
- More injuries to other persons

In other words, both with respect to participant characteristics and to the nature of the incident, gang violence is like gangs themselves, qualitatively different from its non-gang counterpart. And while the same detail of empirical research has yet to be accomplished in Europe, we alluded in an earlier chapter to some findings that have emerged on the continent. Based on 19 European reports from England and Scotland, Norway, Germany, Italy, the Netherlands, France, and Russia, a Eurogang Program Team suggested the following:

1. European violence levels are lower than in the U.S.;
2. Gun violence is also lower. Lesser weapons and fist fighting are most common, although England is now reporting an increase in firearms use, and weapons from Iraq and Afghanistan are now appearing in Europe. Gun homicides are still rare;
3. Because European gangs are commonly less territorial, gang violence motives have less to do with gang rivalries than with ethnic hostilities, group identity and status, and support of other crimes (robbery, extortion, etc.);
4. The victims of gang violence are determined in large part by the motives for the violence. That is, victimization tends to be rational, not "random" or "senseless". The connection to drug trafficking in particular is far lower than is reported in the U.S.

If Euroburg reflects the general European patterns – and there is little reason to expect otherwise – then the panic suggested in reporter van der Waal's initial articles was probably overstated. The ethnographies for The Smokes and Zealots certainly suggest this. The anonymity of The Robber Barons with Andre Mellers' gang unit suggests it as well. Only Conrad's concern about the violence potential of The Old Town Skins stands in contrast. No gang homicides have been reported in the first year of the Euroburg research project, and few serious violent incidents have been reported. The forthcoming youth survey findings thus become the next test of the levels of crime, and violence in particular, among the four gangs identified to date.

29. Youth Survey, Early Results

To: Finn Esbensen esbensenf@umsl.edu

The tremendous work you and your Eurogang working group did on the Youth Survey is beginning to pay off with results from various locations. We can now add Martin Keller's Euroburg Project to that list. I thought I'd share some preliminary results with you. The credit for these goes to Keller's student Liz, a data jock for whom I've developed a lot of respect.

I've asked Liz to run some descriptive analyses for me, even though the return rate from the schools is still only about 60% (using classrooms as the unit, rather than schools or respondents). Other responses will be coming in, especially from the schools near the minority enclaves (mostly Muslim housing developments), but getting cooperation there has not been easy. Keller's assistant, Magda, has connections with the education ministry that are now being invoked with some success and those schools are beginning to resolve the hesitations. If anything, the current bias in the results will underestimate the prevalence of gang members and gang crime, but not the typology and operational comparisons I'm reporting to you.

I've asked Liz, for now, to concentrate on four outcomes:

1. the gang typology questions;

2. the prevalence of gang membership compared for admitted membership versus the results from the Eurogang definitional questions;
3. The levels of self-reported crime for gang and non-gang members (using the admitted membership item, yay or nay, for the time being).
4. The effect of different gang measures on reported crime.

As to the typology, Keller's team had already identified two Muslim-based gangs located on the outskirts of the city. Intensive work using the Eurogang ethnographic guidelines has told us much about them. The first, known as The Smokes, is approaching the status of a Traditional street gang. The second, The Zealots, is clearly a Compressed street gang. In addition, the Eurogang experts' survey revealed a number of other youth groups, only two of which fit within the gang typology. The Robber Barons (T.R.B) is a specialty gang of which the police gang unit was not aware (the juvenile cops knew many of them as individual arrestees, but neither they nor the gang unit had seen the group nature of T.R.B.). O.T.S. (Old Town Skins) is also a specialty gang with no territorial affiliation. While T.R.B. members live mostly in and concentrate on property crimes in an area known as the backwater canals, O.T.S. members come together, often via cell-phone calls, to prey on their victims generally in the downtown areas and subways. Dark-skinned victims are preferred, but the homeless, gays, and occasional Jews also are hassled or attacked.

The point for you, Finn, is that the responses from the youth survey confirm the existence of all four gangs, and the typology items work just fine – those on age range, duration, territoriality, size, sub grouping, crime versatility, and so on. The youth responses confirm the two Specialty gangs, the Compressed gang, and the Traditional gang. Further, other informal youth groups in which various student respondents claim membership do not fit within the typology. The typology works in Euroburg just as well as in Manchester and the several Dutch cities to which it has been applied.

Incidentally, this total of only four street gangs in Euroburg is pretty much in line with what was reported in The Hague, and also in Manchester and Oslo, but far below the reports from London and Amsterdam. The first three are roughly Euroburg's equal in population size, but of course London and Amsterdam are far larger.

Second, Liz has compared the answers of respondents to your question #81 ("Do you consider your group of friends to be a gang?") to their answers to the Eurogang definition questions #64, 66, 71, 78, and 79 (ages, street orientation, durability, and illegal activity). Self admitted gang members (#81) amount so far to nine percent of the total. Those who answer according to the five questions operationalizing the Eurogang definition of gang total to just over five percent (and those fitting under both operations only four percent). Thus the single-item operation used in so much American research – are you a member – and found universally to be "robust" in comparing gang and non-gang attributes is not perhaps as discriminating as our Eurogang operation. Hooray for our side! I'll come back to this at the end of this report.

The Euroburg levels of admitted gang membership are well below those in the U.S., as reported over several years (Denver, 14%; Seattle, 15%; Rochester, 30%; your G.R.E.A.T. study cities, 17%). No surprise in that. The Euroburg 9% can be compared to the admitted levels reported for Bremen by Schumann (9.2%), for Edinburgh by Bradshaw (13%), for Moscow and Kazan by Salagaev et al. (17% and 10%), for Zurich by Haymoz (11.4%), for Sarajevo by Maljevic (5.4%), and for 15 Italian cities by Gatti (16.8% on average). Euroburg may thus be a bit low, although later returns from the schools in the immigrant areas may well shove Euroburg up a few points. Of course, oversampling in higher gang areas in some cases should make us leery of putting too much weight on these comparisons. In any case, it's clear that European policy makers who are denying their gang membership may do so at considerable peril.

What happens when we look at the rates judged by the five Eurogang definition items? As in Euroburg, they come down. Manchester is 6.7% (Medina), the Netherlands is 6% (Weerman), Moscow and Kazan 12% and 6% (Salagaev et al.), Sarajevo less than 6% (Maljevic), and the 15 Italian cities range from 0% to 10.6%, with an average at 6% (Gatti). Edinburgh drops from 13% admitted to 3.3% by a restricted but not Eurogang definition. The only differences in the pattern of results lower than the self-admitted levels are Sarajevo which remained essentially the same and Zurich which went up from 11.2% to 12.9%. however, Haymoz reported that those identified as gang by the combined Eurogang and self-admitted items dropped drastically to 4.6%. Liz hasn't looked at this combined pattern yet, but logically it should always lead to lower levels.

If this survey of other cities isn't complete, I think it's extensive enough to suggest the general levels as lower than in most U.S. cities but high enough that our European friends had better take the problem of gang membership seriously. For my friends in Euroburg, it's now clear that they are neither unique in this respect, nor without counterparts to whom they could turn to discuss common issues.

Now, to the third item on the table: how delinquent are these Eurogang members as judged by your youth survey's self-report items? Liz has gone to items #33 through 47, the 15 item scale. To date, there are far fewer reports to which I can compare the Euroburg results – Bremen, Manchester, Edinburgh, and the Netherlands. In Euroburg, the preliminary grouped comparisons, using a 12-month reporting period, show about a 4 to 1 ratio of overall offending, gang to non-gang youth. The property offense ratio is also about 4 to 1 while violence is 5 to 1 (but of course the overall violence frequencies are far below the property crime frequencies). I've tabulated below for you, as best I can, the approximate figures for the other four locations as well, using their own operational definition of "gang".

	Euroburg	Bremen	Manchester	Netherlands	Edinburgh
Overall	4.0:1	3.1:1	-	4.4:1	4.5:1
Property	4.3:1	3.0:1	3.2:1	6.7:1	-
Violence	2.5:1	6.0:1	2.6:1	4.1:1	3:1

Until I did this exercise, I had little feeling for the generally low variation in self-report ratios across locations. One reason might well be that the bigger gang cities have not yet yielded data; London, Paris, Amsterdam and so on are not in our picture as yet. Yet even in these four locations, gang members far outdistance their non-gang counterparts in illegal involvement.

Euroburg seems to fit right into this mid-sized location pattern. The somewhat lower violence ratio from members of its four gangs is concordant with the ethnographic reports we're getting, and typically lower than the statements from certain public officials and press reports.

The final question I posed to Liz is what happens to the gang/non-gang ratios of we use the two different measures of gang membership. The table above is based on using item #81, self-admitted gang membership. Liz called me two nights ago to report the three ratios using our Eurogang definition items. Reducing the numbers of gang members in this fashion from 9 percent to just over 5 percent of all respondents does, indeed, make a difference. The new figure for overall offending rises to 5.2 to 1, for property crimes 6.0 to 1, and for violence almost to 5.0 to 1, double the earlier figure.

What's happening here? My guess would be that our Eurogang measure excludes a number of group members who overclaim gang membership, who might in the U.S. be labeled "wannabes." That leaves us with more "purified" gang members, similar to what you found in your G.R.E.A.T. evaluation when you used concentric circles to draw out the more committed gang members. If the much-used gang-admission measure is robust, as has indeed been shown dozens of times, then our Eurogang measure is even more so, further distinguishing street gang members from other youth group members of various sorts. Q.E.D.

I'll keep you in touch with further youth survey results as the returns from the missing schools and classes come in and Liz moves to more refined analyses not only of these items but all of the others on the survey as well. She has become very expert in regression analyses and is eager to strut her stuff on these data. The only problem is the usual one of finding continuation funding beyond this first year of the Euroburg Project. My impression is that Martin Keller's political connections will manage this.

30. An Early Report to the Profession

The occasion was the annual convention of the European Society of Criminology, held this year in the early part of September and hosted by the University of Edinburgh. In the late morning of the second day, session #16 was held in the King Malcolm and Saint Margaret lecture hall, recently renovated in the old chapel of the castle. The convention reception had been held the night before, when 700 criminologists were treated to tastings of single malt scotch and the blaring music of the Scots Guards Band and Pipers in the castle courtyard. A session in the old chapel seemed a fitting sequel to the prior night's festivities.

At precisely 10:00 AM, the group was called to order by the panel chairperson, who gave a brief introduction:

Chair: Good morning, everyone, and welcome to session #16 in your program, under the title of New Reports form the Eurogang Program. I may be preaching to the choir, here, as I see many familiar faces in the audience, so I'll be brief. For those of you not yet familiar with the Eurogang Program, it is a consortium of approximately 200 researchers and policy makers who have been collaborating over a ten-year period to develop a prospective, multi-method, multi-site program of research on street gangs. Phase I consisted of the development of common definitions and a set of five research instruments capable of yielding valid and reliable data across many nations. Phase II, the current phase, involves an emphasis on conceptual underpinnings of gang activity, including such topics as violence, urban settings, migration, immigration, and ethnicity. Phase III, barely started but drawing nearer to hand, will be the instituting of genuine cross-national comparative gang research.

Four of the five papers you will hear today are Phase II papers from Dublin, Sarajevo, Barcelona, and Toulouse. The fifth is the description of a new and independent project initiated in response to panicky reports about a local gang problem, but one which quickly incorporated all the components of our Eurogang Program. I warn our five presenters that I will be merciless in adhering to our time limits. With only an hour and a half available to us, I must limit each presentation to 15 minutes. If you finish in under 15 minutes, we can take a question or two in each case. If not, we'll have some time at the end for questions posed to any of the presenters.

The clock starts now, so I'll introduce the independent project's presenter, Professor Martin Keller of the Criminology Institute at the Free University of Euroburg.

Keller: Thank you so much. I am going to describe a truly team effort. The Euroburg Project team, which I lead, includes my trusted administrative assistant, four eager and hard working graduate students, three street workers from the State Ministry of Immigration, and a police sergeant who supervises his department's special gang unit. Two of the graduate students are with us here today and I'll ask them to raise their hands: Heinrich the indefatigable ethnographer and Liz, the admirable data analyst. Thank you both.

Now, here's a sketched map of our city of Euroburg with some of its more distinctive features. In terms of population, Euroburg is similar to such other Eurogang cities as Manchester, Oslo, and The Hague to name a few. Like other such cities, it has had a street gang problem for twenty years or more, but not so serious a problem that officials talked about it very openly. A little over a year ago, however, a series of gang incidents caught the attention of the police and the press, leading to a public forum organized by the mayor. This in turn led to the funding of our project to delve into the prevalence and seriousness of the street gang problem. What I want to do today is provide you with some of our preliminary results, and also comment on the utility of the Eurogang instruments.

We have located four street gangs in Euroburg, and a number of other informal youth groups that do not fit the Eurogang definition of a "durable, street-oriented youth group for which illegal activity is part of its identity". To the north, you will see on the map Fort Araby and The Village. Both are housing developments that include the great bulk of our Muslim populations. Fort Araby is older, reflects the influx of guest workers several decades ago, and is heavily populated by people of Moroccan origin. The street gang there is named The Smokes, comprising what The Maxson/Klein typology labels a Traditional gang. The Village is a newer development, more mixed in national origin, but primarily Turkish with recent refugee bulges from Afghanistan and Iraq. The gang there is known as The Zealots, a smaller and younger group fitting the typology's category of a Compressed gang. These are the two gangs we knew about early on.

Our application of the Eurogang experts' survey revealed two additional street gangs. T.R.B., or The Robber Barons, is located in the southern quadrant, the map area designated as the Backwater Canal District. This is a Specialty gang, as described in the typology, small and composed only of native-born Euroburgers. The fourth gang, O.T.S., or Old Town Skins, has no territorial affiliation, but members make contact by cell phone and gather downtown in Old Town and in the subways where there are relevant immigrants, gay, homeless, and Jewish targets for their predations. Heinrich, whom I introduced to you minutes ago, has been our primary ethnographer in Fort Araby. Others have been doing field work with the three other gangs, always adhering to the ethnographic guidelines of the Eurogang Program.

For those of you interested in female participation in these gangs, I can report that you would come up short in Euroburg, as Liz learned first hand. The two immigrant Muslim gangs actively discourage female gang participation, as do their families. The Skins have no female members, although our field man studying them has noted a number of female companions he describes as "frightening" in their styles and demeanor. Several girls are peripherally involved in the thefts and burglaries that comprise the principal offenses of The Robber Barons.

We are now getting preliminary results from the Eurogang youth survey being used in a large sample of classrooms. They confirm the existence of the four gangs, along with other groups that do not fit the Eurogang definition, although some group members claim their groups to be a gang. This is an important finding. So far, about 9% of respondents claim their group to be a gang, but only 5% describe the groups as required by the more restrictive Eurogang criteria. I'm told that both Dutch and French studies recently have noted a serious "over-claiming" of gang status, while other locations report differences more like ours. Given the relatively few street gangs in Euroburg, and their size, the 9% self-admitted gang figure seems to me unreasonably high; or said another way, thank you for offering the Eurogang definition.

Saying this reminds me that I want to comment on your Eurogang Program. Our panel chair today, sitting over there with his 15 minute clock and the benign smile on his face, has been invaluable in alerting us to the five Eurogang instruments. The ethnographic guidelines are being followed assiduously in our project, providing unusually satisfying comparative data on our four gangs. The youth survey, even before the full returns are in, is allowing Liz to do yeoman work in developing the pictures of gang/non-gang differences; it is also keeping her off the streets, to Heinrich's relief (at which point, an audible "ugh" emanated from the direction of Liz and an even louder "Amen" from Heinrich).

Your city descriptors protocol is guiding some data collection now. However, the process is slow and complex and requires consultation from university colleagues whose expertise is different from ours.

Finally, your prevention/intervention survey, as well constructed as it is, proves inappropriate to Euroburg. It is designed to elicit information about data-based and evaluated gang programs. We have no such thing in Euroburg, and I seriously question how many you will find throughout Europe.

Still, I must tell you that without the Eurogang Program's work on definitions and instruments, we could not possibly have come as far and as fast as we have. We could not possibly have found ourselves positioned to assess the Euroburg gang situation in comparison to that in many other cities. And we wouldn't have had the counsel and guidance of our American consultant, today's panel chair.

Now as a dividend, let me share with you the latest bulletins from Liz. First, Euroburg's rate of admitted gang membership revealed in the youth survey is a bit lower, at least in our returns to date, than those reported in such Eurogang study sites as Bremen, Edinburgh, Moscow, Kazan, Zurich, and fifteen Italian cities. However, the rate as measured by the items operationalizing the Eurogang definition is very similar to most of these other gang locations.

Second, Euroburg's level of self-reported delinquency taken from the youth survey is very similar to the levels in the few sites for which comparable reports are available: Bremen, Manchester, Edinburgh, and the Netherlands. Our property crimes match those in these locations, while our violent crimes are a bit lower, all of this when comparing gang to non-gang responses to the 15-item self-report scale.

Third, Liz has compared these gang to non-gang crime ratios using the self-admitted measure and the more restrictive Eurogang measure of gang membership. Not surprisingly, the gang member ratio goes up when using the more pure Eurogang operationalization. Again, I interpret this as an advantage to the Eurogang approach over the more common self-admission approach to gang membership.

There are other things I'd like to discuss with you about our project, such as some serious ethical concerns and recommendations for policy, but under the time constraints on our panel, I'll defer these for now. I will be taking them up with our local officials in Euroburg. I thank you for inviting our presentation today, Mr. Chairman, and I appreciate the attention of your audience.

Chair: Thank you, my friend. I must tell our audience that I have thoroughly enjoyed my visits to your city, including the time I've spent with team members like Liz and Heinrich. My watch tells me we have time for a question or two. Yes – the young man in the back of the room. Please tell us who you are and where you are from.

Questioner: My name is Hans Kersten, and I'm a graduate student in Frankfurt. My question is actually for Heinrich. I've been asked by my professor to undertake a field study of Turkish gang members in Frankfurt. Obviously, I hope to use the ethnographic guidelines from the Eurogang Program, but I'm concerned about my ability to achieve rapport with the Turkish kids. I'm a native-born German and I don't speak their language. How did you gain entrée to The Smokes in Euroburg?

Heinrich: Man, that's a question with a lot of answers. I think we need to talk about it over some beer later today. Also, you should read the chapter by Hermann Tertilt in The Eurogang Paradox, the first book to come out of the Eurogang Program. He studied a group like yours in Frankfurt and describes the process. I'll say just a few things here. I spent a lot of time at the beginning just hanging around Fort Araby, and especially at a café and coffee bar where a number of the older Smokes hung out. Liz was with me on a number of those occasions, but I got closer when she wasn't with me. I was very honest and direct about my purposes. I identified myself as a graduate student, usually carried a book bag with books and papers, and sometimes I had my laptop, which was an ice-breaker. The important thing was being honest, and being a good listener. Most of The Smokes were bi-lingual, which helped me a lot. I'll bet most of your Turkish kids will speak German – don't worry about the language.

But I have to tell you that over more than a year, I still don't feel totally comfortable with my group, I don't think I have everyone's trust, and I know they're keeping things from me. It can't be helped. Also, after an incident that was interpreted by Professor Keller and other team members as a threat to my safety, I was teamed up with another graduate student, a guy who grew up in Amsterdam and had a lot of exposure to Moroccans there. He's made it easier for me and watches my back. You should consider a "buddy system" for your work in Frankfurt.

Chair: Ok, thank you Hans for the question and Heinrich for the response. I'd like to hear your beer-laden conversation later today. Now we'll move on to the next presentation.

Whatever the nature of that later conversation between Hans and Heinrich might have been, no one else was there to listen in. This was old home week for the American consultant with many of his Eurogang colleagues, American and European alike. Their choice was dinner and wine and companionship in one of Edinburgh's finer restaurants on Princes Street. Professor Keller took his favorite student Liz to a local pub where they were joined by Mrs. Keller, fresh from her tour of local art and craft shops: fish and chips, haggis, shepherd's pie, trifle, and locally brewed ale.

31. Report to the Mayor's Panel

The early morning autumn mist gave an eerie feel to the town square. It was quiet and empty as Dirk and Conrad crossed by the Neptune statue. Liz came out the front door of St. Agnes Cathedral and joined them as they moved toward town hall to hear the city fathers and Professor Keller discuss the project findings and implications. As they passed McDonald's, open for breakfast, Dirk and Conrad both pointed to the side wall, freshly painted to cover up old political graffiti and tags. But even more fresh were the gang tags – Dirk guessed they were only hours old – O.T.S. in black spray paint, Smokes in grey, both in fancy block letters. More worrisome were the black lines crossing out Smokes. O.T.S. was making a statement, Conrad noted with some displeasure. Liz merely shrugged; she had seen this sort of thing before. There had been no O.T.S./Smokes clashes according to Sgt. Mellers. "Boys will be boys," she said to her comrades.

They met Alexander, Abu, and Muzafer on the steps of town hall and passed through the maze of flags and paintings to the council chamber upstairs. Magda had saved a row of seats for them all; only Heinrich was not yet present. Keller and Mellers were talking behind the dais, soon joined by a few other original members of the mayor's panel. Present were Chief

Schmidt, the City Accountant, the chief security officer of the city schools department, the director of the city youth commission, the state immigration ministry's representative, and the mayor.

Those present were balanced in numbers by those absent: the two city council members, the head of the Council of Euroburg Businessmen, the deputy director of the school system, the priest and the not-for-profit agency director, and the lawyer from the young adults' court. To the side of the dais were a few assistants and reporter Patrick van der Waal.

The mayor waited for 15 minutes for other panel members to appear, but they did not. Nor was there a large audience. The fog and the absence of the market stalls in the square took their toll, but the mayor suggested another source of the low turnout:

"I appreciate seeing you all here this morning," he said with smiling optimism. "The smaller group than we were a year or more ago reflects, I trust, the quieter period of youth or gang crime we are experiencing in our city. Would you say, Chief, that we have achieved a reduction in gang crime and therefore in community concerns with the problem?"

The Chief merely nodded and pointed over to Andre. "Our intelligence," reported the sergeant, "certainly suggests a quieter period on the streets. We've learned a lot more about our gangs over the past year and are better able to keep a lid on them."

The mayor turned to Keller: "Then perhaps, Professor, you and your research team, funded through our office, deserve credit for this return to normalcy after last year's outbreak."

Keller: "Thank you, your honor, for the suggestion. I'd love to take credit for the downturn, but then I'd properly have to share the credit with my team members out in the audience there, and then there wouldn't be enough left for me." The panelists' chuckles were rewarding, but he then followed up with a reminder: "The history of street gang activity has been shown by criminologists here and abroad to be a matter of repeated cycles. Almost regardless of what we do to, with, or for street gangs, their activity levels go up and down over time. Taking credit for a downturn may only set us up for public ridicule when the cycle turns upward again. Gang research and gang intervention are not areas that should breed much optimism."

The mayor: "Well, I'm not sure that's what I wanted to hear, so why don't we turn the meeting over to you now, Professor, to understand what your university team has learned and where you think we should go at this point."

The panelists sat back, the audience leaned forward, and Martin Keller, public lecturer, set down his pipe and took up his microphone.

"Let me say first that, while we have reached the end of our first and very substantially funded contract period, our research is not yet completed but is ongoing at a very productive rate. Many thanks go to the members of my team, and I'll ask them to stand and be recognized. All but one, I see, woke up early enough to be here. Also, I should point out that Sgt. Mellers on the panel here has been a part-time member of the team as well, and we've had a good deal of input from an American consultant connected to a large consortium of researchers in what is known as the Eurogang Program.

"Just over a week ago, I presented the preliminary findings of our research to a gathering of the European Society of Criminology. I won't bother you with the details of that research presentation because my charge here this morning is to open some discussion about the public policy issues. However, copies of the paper I presented to the E.S.C. are stacked up at the end of the table there, and I hope you will each take a copy when we're through. I seem to have brought more than were needed this morning: take two!

"What I want to do is inform you briefly about our Euroburg street gangs, and then ask a set of questions – rhetorical questions in some cases – to set some parameters for your policy discussions. We have identified four street gangs currently active in the city, two small and two rather large. The two smaller groups call themselves The Robber Barons, because of their concentration on thefts and burglaries, and the Old Town Skins, a fairly typical skinhead, supremacist group. Both are composed primarily of native-born Euroburgers. By way of contrast the two larger gangs, of longer duration and residents mostly of the Middle East area on the outskirts, are composed mostly of second and third generation immigrant Muslim origin. In one case, located in Fort Araby, they are predominantly Moroccan and in the other, located in The Village, they are predominantly Turkish with a recent influx of Afghan and Iraqi refugees.

"I think most of our discussion must be about these larger, immigrant-based groups. Given sufficient police intelligence about The Robber Barons and the Skins, I believe Sgt. Mellers and his unit can either contain or even eliminate them as serious problems. But the other two groups are not easily dismissed. Given that prelude, here then are the questions I want to pose to you.

"Number one: What is gang reality? That is, how do we know what any city's gang problem is? In this case, the police didn't know one of these groups, TRB, existed, and didn't consider the second one – the O.T.S. – to be a real gang. Small businessmen in their area knew about T.R.B. but not the others. School officials reported mostly on groups in their areas only, including a number that were not street gangs. Press reports were third-hand, not even second-hand, and more misleading than informative. We came to our conclusion about four street gangs through a combination of surveys of local informants, a review of police files, a large-scale survey of students throughout the city, and field observations by trained university-based researchers.

"Number two: Is Euroburg unique? The simple answer is no. We've spent some time reviewing the street gang situation in other European cities roughly comparable to ours in size. We have the same types of gangs, although perhaps fewer than in some cases. The crime level as well is similar to that in these other cities. The immigrant gang situation, in particular, is very similar, regardless of whether the minority population is Moroccan or Turkish or Algerian or Pakistani or Jamaican or Chinese or what have you. It is marginal social status, not the specific ethnicity, that holds the clue to much of Europe's gang development.

"Number three: is the problem 'them,' or 'us,' or both? Put another way, should gangs be conceptualized as a crime problem – a matter for the police and courts, or as a community problem – a matter for all of us? I submit to you that to the extent that most gangs emerge from minority communities, and may even receive support in those communities, then to that extent we must share the credit. It takes a majority to create a minority. There is an intersection between the two that yields the present situation.

"Number four: Whose kids are these, anyway? Gang members are our children, whether native-born or immigrants. Is there any parent in this audience who intentionally ignores his or her child? I think not. But as a city, we are ignoring many of our children, turning them into social isolates. This need not be the case.

"So to you, Mr. Mayor, and to the members of our panel, I want to suggest ---"

At which point, Keller was interrupted by the Chief's cell phone ringing. As he raised the phone to his ear, André Mellers' phone went off, and almost simultaneously a uniformed officer came through the side door of the council chamber, crossed rudely in front of Keller and handed a note to the Sergeant. He read it and looked at the Chief who nodded at him. He rose and followed the officer down an aisle through the audience. He paused briefly at the row of seats occupied by the research team, looked at Liz and pursed his lips, then strode on through the back door.

Liz swiveled to watch him go, turned visibly pale, and rose quickly to follow him. As panel members whispered to each other and the audience chattered noisily, Magda also rose to follow Liz. Then Patrick van der Waal closed his laptop, pocketed his cell pone and headed out a side door. For once in his life, Martin Keller was at a loss, looking truly bewildered.

The mayor, after a whisper from the Chief, rescued Keller: "I'm not sure what has happened here just now," he said loudly enough to force silence in the room, "but it's clear that our attention is no longer focused on the final comments from Professor Keller. I will ask him to provide us with a written version of today's presentation, with a view toward what steps we ought to be considering. Prof. Keller, and everyone here, thank you so much for your attendance today. I declare the panel meeting adjourned."

The exits were quickly made, except for the remaining members of the research team. Alexander said to them simply, "It has to be Heinrich," and they too left. Martin Keller remained alone, with the task of gathering up all his copies of the E.S.C. report to return them to the Institute, unread. He put them in a large box, lifted it in both arms and headed for the back door. He forgot his pipe, sitting next to his still open microphone.

32. Dealing With It

From the Euroburg Daily News, September 23, by Patrick van der Waal

MAYOR'S GANG PANEL INTERRUPTED BY ASSAULT REPORT

In the midst of a report by Professor Martin Keller to the Mayor's panel on gang crime yesterday morning, emergency cell phone calls and written messages disrupted the proceedings. After a year of study, the professor was describing his research team's progress in assessing the serious nature of street gang crime in Euroburg. As he prepared to outline the policy implications to a group of public officials, the emergency messages forced a halt in the proceedings and the Mayor adjourned the meeting in the council chambers of Town Hall.

This reporter has learned that the emergency was the brutal beating late Sunday night of Heinrich Cutler, 24, a field observer on Professor Keller's research team. According to Sergeant André Mellers of the police gang unit, Mr. Cutler was found unconscious in a downtown side street by city street cleaners. He was transported to the hospital where he is currently in the intensive care unit following surgery for head wounds, broken bones, and removal of his spleen. Hospital personnel report his condition as very critical; he is in a "deep coma" according to a hospital spokeswoman.

Meanwhile, police have identified a principal suspect in the assault, 24-year-old Sarkand Kazakh who also goes by the street name of "Samurai." Kazakh is a resident of the Fort Araby housing development and a reported leader of a street gang known as The Smokes. According to Sgt. Mellers, Kazakh was also a suspect in the beating last year of another street worker associated with the Keller research team. A warrant for Kazakh's arrest has been issued, but he has not been seen since the assault on Mr. Cutler. It is believed he may have fled the country for his family's homeland in the Far East. Interpol and eastern border patrols have been alerted to his status as a fugitive.

From the Euroburg Daily News, September 25, by Patrick van der Waal

SEARCH FOR GANG SUSPECT CONTINUES

At a brief press conference yesterday, the Mayor and Deputy Mayor reported that every possible effort is being made to apprehend the gang member suspected as the assailant, or principal assailant, of Heinrich Cutler, the young researcher assigned to The Smokes street gang. Informants in his gang and in the Fort Araby housing development, have assured police that fugitive Sarkand Kazakh, also known as "Samurai," has fled the area. His family has also been questioned about his possible whereabouts, but no further information has emerged. Border patrol officers in several eastern countries reported having seen several individuals similar to Kazakh prior to being alerted to the search for him, but Euroburg police officials say no firm identifications have been made.

The Deputy Mayor reported at the press conference that the research project in which victim Cutler was involved is continuing and must not be compromised by the incident. Mr. Cutler remains in a deep coma; doctors will not predict the results of their surgery or ongoing treatment regimen. Had he been found earlier, they admit, his chances would be better.

From the Euroburg Daily News, September 29, by Patrick van der Waal

NEW SUSPECTS IN GANG ASSAULT CASE

The police have announced a dramatic development in the case of the severe beating of gang researcher Heinrich Cutler, who remains in a deep coma, with no change in his condition since emergency surgery a week ago. Three suspects in the assault have been arrested, one adult and two minors.

Police would not identify the three, except to say that they were documented members of a Euroburg street gang. Police sergeant André Mellers, in making the announcement, expressed extreme confidence in the arrests; "We have secret intelligence, as well as several forms of physical evidence, that tie these suspects to Mr. Cutler's beating," he reported, adding, "We are being very thorough about this. Mr. Cutler was well known to us as a dedicated researcher. Doing his job well should not have put him in harm's way."

Sgt. Mellers also reported that Mr. Cutler's parents have arrived in Euroburg and are now at his bedside, sharing time there with his life partner and research partner (who has asked not to be identified in press reports). Mr. Cutler's fellow researchers are continuing their project as best they can, I have learned from Professor Martin Keller, the team leader. "But," noted Prof. Keller, "it's hard for us to concentrate on the job when we don't know if this fine young man and friend will recover or pass on."

On the same day this last van der Waal report was published, a special staff meeting was called in the Institute's conference room. Everyone was there, including Liz, to hear a report from André Mellers.

Keller: "Ok, please hold your questions for a few minutes. There has been no change in Heinrich's condition – I just spoke with his father at the hospital – but it's important that you hear what André told me just a little while ago. André ---"

"Thank you. I know you've all seen this morning's report in the paper. I'm gonna tell you everything we know at this point. To start off, we now know that The Smokes had nothing to do with this, nothing at all."

"Hot damn," broke in Dirk. "I want to keep working with them. But what about Samurai?"

"He's no longer a suspect," said André. "We were misled by the affair with Abu over there, by the fact that he had threatened Heinrich, and by his disappearance. We still don't know where he is, and we don't care. Maybe he took off because he thought he'd be blamed. Who's gonna miss him?

"Our suspects – and we know we've got the right guys – are all O.T.S. members (at which point everyone turned toward Conrad who remained expressionless). How do we know?

"One: somebody, a confidential informant, dropped a dime on one of them. That's an old American phrase meaning a phone tip (Again, everyone looked at Conrad, but got nothing in return).

"Two: We checked that name on our clique board at the station. This kid is closely tied to the two others.

"Three: There was evidence at the crime scene, bits of clothing and boot marks on Heinrich's face and hands, that could be tied to the eventual suspects.

"Four: We got a report from a private physician. He had treated an adolescent male for bruises and abrasions he said were sustained in a soccer match. When this doctor read van der Waal's reports, he put two and two together and called our headquarters with the youngster's name. Headquarters gave the name to me, and it was the same as the one we got from the confidential informant.

"Five: With all that, we confronted the boy and his family. The mother retrieved some torn clothing at our request, and the father turned on the boy. We got a confession and the name of his two fellow assailants, the two names we already had on the clique board.

"That's it, except I believe we can guess at the motive. We never let on to this, but the side street where Heinrich was found is just a half a block away from Euroburg's smaller old synagogue. Did you people know Heinrich is Jewish?"

Everyone gasped – "no," "never," "Is Cutler a Jewish name?" and so on. All but Liz and Magda, who said almost in unison, "Of course."

"And so what," asked Liz.

And André responded, "So these guys came across him in the late evening outside the synagogue, and also recognized him as the guy working closely with The Smokes. According to the older of the three Skins, who bragged about it to one of my officers, 'Kill a Jew and blame an Arab; it's two for one'."

"My God, that's terrible," blurted Magda. And Liz, now in tears, whispered, "I don't get it. I just don't get it. What's wrong with these people?"

"I get it," responded Conrad. "I was there once, remember? I was a Skinhead, I was a gang member. Don't look at it from your own viewpoint; get into their heads."

"Yeah," agreed André, "and that's what I've been learning from all this time on the project. As a cop, I could just demonize these guys and let it go at that. No need to understand. And you Liz – I really feel for you. I know it's rough. I deal with victims' families and friends all the time. Their grief can block out their understanding. You're a fine young woman and I've come to understand that Heinrich is a fine young man, even if he doesn't love us cops. But I guess it's not just good guys and bad guys."

"And that," broke in the professor, "that is what we need to discuss. What went on in that side street beyond good and evil? My guess is that three people confronted one, but knowing that one to be our Heinrich, he wouldn't have backed off, turned to walk the other way. And the three wouldn't have known how to back off, given each other's presence. There's a phrase – 'pluralistic ignorance' – that describes this. Each person in an upcoming event wants to get out of it, but assumes the others don't. Each assumes he's unique, and unless someone explicitly expresses doubt, they all continue down the path that none, in fact, want to take. Yablonsky described this well in the gang beating of a young polio victim in New York. It took place at the end of a long trek into a rival gang's territory; few wanted to go, but each thought all the others did. In such a group, you would lose face by questioning the action. The young polio victim ended up dead.

"Liz, consider the very data you and the others have been gathering. You've seen that gang members reveal differences in the youth survey from other youth not in gangs, including those involved in other kinds of groups. If I remember your initial report of such differences, gang members are drawn together by things like negative events in their lives, lower parental monitoring, family members in trouble with the law, lower commitment to school, exposure to violence in their neighborhoods, and dependence on age peers. Being drawn toward each other makes them more vulnerable to group processes, like this pluralistic ignorance."

The American consultant had remained silent throughout the meeting. Heinrich was their friend, the team was their team, and he was quite aware of his outsider status. Still, this group process discussion was his meat. He addressed the whole group, not just Liz:

"Remember some of those group processes we've discussed before. Gang members tend to share a feeling of being socially marginalized even before they join the gang. This feeling can then be reinforced within the group. They develop an oppositional culture as a group defense against outside pressures and interventions. All this gets increased by shared acceptance of anti-social norms, including the commission of illegal acts and the rhetoric of violence."

Alexander interrupted: "And you're saying this about these three Skinheads, but it applies to everything we've seen in The Village. Three Zealots, or three Smokes, might have ended up in the same situation if they came upon a juicy target like Heinrich. I understand that now. Remember what happened in the subway to Abu. This group process stuff you talk about can really take over – like you said, group process trumps ethnicity."

"Exactly; lots of experience in the street supports this, regardless of whether it's in my Los Angeles or the gang cities of Europe. Heinrich's fate is just a by-product of all this. Don't look at something about Heinrich for the answer; look at the group phenomenon. From that point of view, it doesn't matter whether he was attacked by Samurai and his Smokes or by Old Town Skins."

No counter-arguments were offered in the conference room. There was only silence as everyone understood that their tragedy with Heinrich was part and parcel of the kind of research topic they had selected for themselves.

Finally, it was Liz who moved the ball forward. "Ok," she said. "I accept all that, of course. But how do we get this into the Professor's discussions with the Mayor and his people? He's supposed to give them ideas for policy, or programs – something beyond police crackdowns and parent training, to use two irrelevant examples."

The American responded. "Actually, I'm not willing to leave out your two examples any more than a host of others. I like to recommend things that have been tested and proven useful. And there's the rub, of course. The American experience has been relatively devoid of proven-useful gang programs – emphasis on proven – and worse yet, devoid of programs that take group process and gang structure into account. My colleague Cheryl Maxson and I looked at about 60 programs across America – prevention programs, intervention programs, suppression programs – and found only six of them that attempted to incorporate knowledge of group process in their designs. Only two of the six included adequate outcome evaluations. Both of these reported no success or even negative outcomes. Not a single program dealt explicitly with variations in gang structure. That doesn't give us much by way of guidelines for Martin to suggest to the Mayor. I've said it before: practitioners and researchers alike tend to forget that gangs are groups.

"On the other hand, very very few of the 60 programs were adequately evaluated in any case, so we can't discard most of them as bearing no promise. We are pretty ignorant about what does and doesn't work. In that sense, anything is fair game.

"I wish I could tell you about some better models here in Europe, but I can't. Martin and I have discussed the gang control programs we've learned of. There are small gang prevention programs in Stockholm and Frankfurt, but they don't deal explicitly with group issues. There are gang intervention programs in Stockholm, Berlin, and Stuttgart that sound as though they should be oriented toward group processes, but don't seem to think in these terms. And there are police intelligence and suppression operations in London, Manchester, Frankfurt, Berlin, Stuttgart, Stockholm, and Copenhagen, but like the Euroburg gang unit, they take little account of group processes and no account of gang structures.

"I should add that clique structures like André's are found in Stockholm as well. That, at least, is a start, but of course it's mostly for criminal intelligence and investigation purposes – an adjunct to suppression.

"So, Liz, the door is open in the policy area. This research team is in a position to talk to officials here in Euroburg about experimenting with reasonable-sounding programs and policies. You're also in a position to argue for the funds to carry out scientific evaluations of these programs. Get these people to talk about their goals, and then activities that tie directly to those goals, and then procedures to implement and sustain those activities over time. It may be too late for this in the U.S. It's not too late here. That's one of the reasons we initiated the Eurogang Program 10 years ago."

Said Prof. Keller, "All right, we'll be discussing all these issues in the months ahead, as we continue to wrap up our data collection and analysis. We're in discussions to get continuation funds to support our efforts. We have our big gala dinner coming up soon – perhaps we'll know more about it then, and more about Heinrich's status as well. Today's meeting has been pretty stressful, and I'm aware that Magda's eyes have been aiming darts at me. Let's quit now. We have plenty to think about before we meet next week. Thank you all. I'm very proud of this group."

Keller reached in his jacket pocket for his pipe, but its loss had not yet yielded a replacement. He was being eased away from his empty addiction, and neither his wife nor Magda had any intention of feeding it.

33. Communities and Gangs

At Alexander's invitation, the three had joined him for a walking tour – Martin Keller, the American consultant, and the deputy mayor. "This will be my seminar," Alexander chortled. It was a crisp autumn morning. There were yellow and brown leaves clinging to their perches, and chestnuts scattered about the sidewalks. A good day for a walk, a good day for a "seminar," and a good day to gang up on the deputy mayor.

They met at the central station and took the subway to the Akbar station. From there, the spur line took them to the terminus in the "Middle East." Alexander led them first to the west and the four looming towers of Fort Araby. As they entered the common grounds between the towers it grew darker, and colder; the sun did not reach in, and the breezes stiffened into a chilly, swirling wind.

The first sights were of barred windows on the first two floors, communal garbage bins – some open, some not – many the home away from home for stray cats and scrawny dogs whose heritages were undeterminable. Alexander pointed to some windows that were boarded over, apartments abandoned and available for squatters "and Smokes," noted Alexander. He led them inside the western-most tower. The door was open beyond the security screen that hung loosely on one hinge. The corridor was dark, but not enough to hide The Smokes' graffiti and individual tags, many of them faded over the years of inattention. Unlike the odors of the garbage bins outside, there was a strong hint of charcoal and cooking lamb, a mixture of spices that might, in aggregate, be taken for curry sauce.

But the cooks were not visible. No one was visible. The corridors were empty, the dark stairs echoed to their feet, and apartment doors contained no invitations. The deputy mayor complained of a headache, and the need to return outdoors. As they exited, women's and children's faces peered out at them through windows and bars, but no one spoke; more inspectors doing nothing, they may have thought. No need for them to "inspect" the other towers. They were replicas, with different dark faces peering out at the same sunless common grounds. Alexander's "seminar" was Socratic, containing only questions.

"Do you see why my parents left this place for The Village and beyond?"

"Why does a city build such places?"

"If native Euroburgers lived here, do you think Fort Araby would look like this?"

"Do you understand why youth living here will leave this behind and go gangbanging in town?"

The walk eastward to The Village took less than thirty minutes, and thankfully it was in the sun, as was the mostly low-rise Village. The central market was open and busy, a mélange of shops, Village residents, and Euroburgers seeking exotic foods and bargains. A busy place in the sun, surrounded by drab but not darkened apartments. The graffiti were here too, fresher ones for The Zealots along with a few political items which Alexander translated as Turkish, Kurdish, Afghan and Iraqi pride and hate. He led his guests through the maze of the market, picking out a few delicacies for them to taste. He had them look at the names in the apartment entryways, indicating the relative diversity of national origins. They toured a few hallways and peeked into a few apartments, most crowded with women and children. "A nicer 'slum,'" he said sardonically. He identified a few knots of adolescents as gang or nongang, mixing easily with both sorts: "Sasha Pasha, Pasha Sasha," called out one youngster.

"It really is a village," Alexander pointed out," but it's a damned crowded one whose people are the only resource. There's the soccer pitch and an informal coffee house, but otherwise a lot of young guys are on their own, just as they are in Forty Araby. They hang with each other 'cause that's what available – that and taking the subway downtown to look for targets."

One of the older Zealots was introduced by Alexander, name of Hussein, who bore the scars of several Smokes/Zealots confrontations. The deputy mayor asked him, "Wouldn't it be better to avoid fights with The Smokes, and have peace conversations with them instead?"

Hussein responded as if trained in street gang rhetoric: "No, man; you win the last fight, then you conversate!"

Alexander led them away quickly; Hussein had fulfilled his purpose, capping the tour of the Middle East with the clear reminder that communities spawn gangs. They returned to the subway, took it all the way back to the central station, and then headed up into Old Town, across a canal bridge and on along the canal toward the old district of guild halls and merchants' homes from centuries past. Alexander pointed out that he now lived just north of this district, as did some other third generation immigrant families. "We don't have to live in the Middle East," he said pointedly. "We can live here privately, honor our family traditions and pray toward Mecca in the east regularly. Nobody bothers us."

And that gave the American consultant his opening. As they walked along the canal and past the piers, he turned to the deputy mayor. "Sir, if you will allow me a little lecture time, I'd like to comment on the multiple communities that make up a city like Euroburg. It's not the city that might change the gang situation here; it's the communities. You know a lot more about the nature of Euroburg than I could ever hope to. But at the same time, I know something about the nature of communities that spawn gangs and support gangs, however inadvertently.

"A colleague of mine provided a great quote. She said, 'It's as if the community context is taken as a given, as an unalterable element in the panoply of gang risk.' The result is that we try to change gang members themselves, but seldom think about altering the local context that surrounds them. But think about our tour of Fort Araby and The Village this morning. If they produce a gang problem, should we just try to change the gang, or should we also look much more closely at the neighborhood, the community.

"I felt very closed in, very surrounded by the denseness of those two communities, and I was just a visitor. Imagine how it is for many of the permanent residents, especially for youngsters trying to spread their wings. Their homes – often crowded and disadvantaged – are nested in a block or a multi-unit structure having similar homes. Each of these small areas is nested in a low or poorly serviced neighborhood; the neighborhood is nested in a marginalized community, usually with strong ethnic overlays. Does it make sense to count on Alexander and his various one-on-one relationships to bring about change, or do we need to place his efforts in a sea of broader social changes?

"Look at these old guild houses along the canal, especially the ones now converted into private apartments. The community feeling here – to the extent there is one – is going to be vastly different from what we sensed this morning. We can describe such contrasting communities in terms of structural elements, all the way from schools and soccer pitches down to garbage disposal. We can look at differences in community efficacy, as it is called, the capacity of the residents to cohere around and deal together with their problems. We can try to understand what different ethnicities or national origins bring to the table, what the different youth groups and gang structures provide as targets for intervention, and how ingrained in the community the gangs have become.

"My point, of course, is that communities or neighborhoods have lots of entry points for trying to bring about change. You and your fellow city officials actually have a lot more leverage for change then you may think. Let me put it as dramatically as I can. You and the mayor and the city council and your municipal agencies might think about two different types of communities here in Euroburg.

"One of these is featured by economic disadvantage, population density, residential instability, ethnic isolation, family disruptions, low employment opportunities, and a sense of little hope for the youth growing up there.

"The other displays collective efficacy with social cohesion, resident networks, mutual trust in neighbors to intervene in troublesome situations, and so on. One sees informal social control and neighborhood empowerment, and shared values that suggest there is hope in life. There are connections between community residents and various assets and resources, both private and municipal. There are people like Alexander empowered to foster such connections on behalf of youth and their families, so that something other than dependence on a gang culture is available.

"Please excuse the moral crusade in what I'm saying. It's just that I know communities are not fixed entities. In the gang arena, they are challenges to be understood and manipulated for change ---

At this point, having walked well into the mixed residential area beyond the canal and the old merchants' area, Martin Keller broke in to continue the ganging up on the poor deputy mayor whose heart was in the right place but who was not used to being targeted by academic protagonists.

"I see quite a few empty old homes and others broken into apartments with rental signs along these streets," Keller opened. "Filling these with low income but working immigrant families – perhaps like Alexander's – is one of a number of specifics I hope to include in my formal policy report to the mayor. I'm going to suggest that the Old Town Skins and The Robber Barons be left to the police for the most part. They are what the American researchers call 'specialty gangs,' for which law enforcement procedures seem quite appropriate and successful. My main concern is with the situation in Fort Araby and The Village."

They had settled into an outdoor café near the entrance to the castle gardens now. Three beers and a glass of local red wine were brought to the table, and luncheon menus briefly halted the conversation. But not for long, as the deputy mayor turned to Keller to ask about specific recommendations in his report. They included the following as areas for social planning:

1. Destroy Fort Araby, literally. Examples of reconstituted developments can be found in Manchester, London, New York, Chicago, and other locations.
2. Initiate a low-cost housing program north of the canal; refurbish and upgrade housing in the backwater canals area; purchase and place low-cost housing west of the "houseboat suburbs."
3. Review school curricula to diminish the tracking of immigrant youth into only vocational and technical programs; increase language skills training; introduce comparative culture and religions programs; develop "diversity training" for teachers and administrators.
4. Open the remaining guilds and the unions to non-restrictive apprentice and trainee programs; expand city service jobs in low-cost housing areas.
5. Greatly expand outreach worker programs, not for gangs per se, but as neighborhood street workers connecting youth and families to public and private resources.
6. Seek a permanent local office of immigration affairs to be established by the State ministry of immigration.
7. Establish several municipal service centers (welfare, health, housing, employment) in low-cost housing areas.
8. Work with the Free University school of education to develop educational enrichment projects for primary and early secondary grades.
9. Collaborate with the Free University to establish minority scholarships and incentives to enroll at the university.
10. Build a modest, modern soccer stadium near Bomber Mountain and easily accessible from the Grand Park subway station.

Keller concluded, noting that other recommendations would be forthcoming, including of course funds to initiate research to evaluate the implementation and outcomes of such programs as were recommended by the mayor's office. With the gang project beginning to wind down, he urged that his suggestions receive the earliest possible attention before momentum was lost. As community tour and lunch finally came to an end, the four participants moved across the bridge to the town square where they prepared to go their separate ways. Keller reminded them of the upcoming "gala dinner" scheduled for the banquet hall in the Roman Museum the following week. It would be the terminal celebration for the first year of the research project, a "town and gown" gathering to celebrate a unique collaboration between the city and its university, and (he hoped) a springboard into a second fruitful year.

They all assured him of their attendance, and shook hands goodbye after a wearying tour and lecture. As the deputy mayor headed toward the entrance to town hall, the other three watched him carefully, hoping for some magical sign that the winds of change would carry him to a sustained effort to bring change to Euroburg.

34. The Gala Dinner

It was Magda who selected the site for the "gala dinner" that would cap off the first year of the project. Several months earlier, arrangements had been made to hold the celebration at The Roman Museum, close to the city square and the canal. It would still be a celebration, but handled with a muffled sense of pride and accomplishment in view of the continuing uncertainty of Heinrich's status.

The museum was a replica of a small Roman villa, even with some struggling Mediterranean umbrella pines lining the entrance walk along the pond. The three floors served different functions. Upstairs there was a film room, a seminar hall with three small break-out rooms, and an antiquities library maintained jointly with the university's classics department. The displays were on the ground floor. Room one contained a walk-around, extended model of a Roman villa from the second century A.D. Room two reconstructed what it was thought the original army encampment along the north side of the river would have looked like. It was half imagined and half based on archaeological digs here and elsewhere. Room three contained, in less than logical order, most of the artifacts found in excavations in several Euroburg sites. There were pieces of sculpture and columns, oil lamps, coins, combs, jewelry, small and large metal and glass containers, amphorae of various sizes, and a collection of military items.

The basement contained several storage rooms and two archaeological workrooms where restorers could be viewed behind glass working at benches in front of numerous storage cabinets. On this night, only one restorer was at work, cataloging what appeared to be ceramic dinnerware – not for the gala dinner, but someone's dinner two millennia earlier perhaps.

The largest room on this floor was the luncheon room, converted on occasions such as this into a medium sized banquet room. Leaving one's coat on the hallway rack, one entered the room to find eight circular dinner tables, beautifully appointed, with large potted plants placed strategically around them. The walls were covered with blow-up photos of excavation sites, separated by plaster of paris columns and temple friezes. There was, indeed, a sense of history here – Euroburg's history, Magda's preferred history.

Each table was set with six chairs and full banquet-style place settings. List of guests names were to be found at each table.

Table 1: Keller and his wife, the American consultant and his wife, the Deputy Mayor and his wife.

Table 2: Andre, Dirk, Conrad, Alexander, Abu, and Muzafer.

Table 3: The university rector, the mayor and his wife, the police chief, Magda and the city accountant.

Table 4 and 5: Members of the mayor's panel from the schools, city council, churches, immigration, and so on.

Table 6: Faculty members who had assisted the project as consultants.

Tables 7 and 8: University staff members, other graduate students, and reporter Patrick van der Waal.

There were two surprises in the lists. The American consultant's wife broke away from her research agenda in Stockholm to fly down to Euroburg and meet her husband's new friends and tour his new city. But the greater surprise was when Magda walked in hand-in-hand with her long-mysterious partner – the city accountant. She answered the question that no one had dared ask. The surprise was a mixed one for Martin Keller – the specter of a conflict of interest loomed before him. At some point in the future, a difficult conversation would be necessary.

But that would be then, and this was now. The guests entered the hall remarkably on time, located their allotted tables, chatted and looked about, and seated themselves. As they did so, two uniformed waiters began to rearrange the potted plants, some of which were very heavy. One pulled and pushed, the other supervised. To do this in the midst of serving starters struck everyone as odd, but they ended up adding their own aesthetic views on the best locations for the various plants.

When the aesthetics were completed, Keller rose, offered his thanks to everyone for their participation, and introduced the rector. He in turn gave a brief, appropriate, and sincere statement about the importance of the relationship between the university and its city, citing the Euroburg Project as a superior example of "town and gown" collaboration.

Keller again rose, with pipe in hand, to acknowledge the American consultant and thank him for his gift of a new pipe. "I should add," he said, "how grateful my wife and Magda are for this gift. My new pipe, made of solid chestnut wood, is just that – solid. The pipe stem is not hollow, but solid. My pipe is a smokeless pipe. I can't puff it, only clench it."

Following applause led vigorously by the two women, Keller went on to say that two oral presentations had been given on the preliminary results of the project, and a third, policy-oriented report would soon be available and delivered to the mayor and his panel.

The mayor, on cue, then rose to say that the report would receive his immediate attention and be considered seriously by the panel. He was grateful, he reported, for the university's work on behalf of the city and was pleased to announce the availability of funds to continue the work through a second year.

This time the applause was thunderous. Tables one and two arose in unison to lead the charge. Keller expressed his gratitude and pleasure on behalf of his team. He then set down his pipe, waited for full attention and reported on the one topic almost everyone was afraid to face.

"Before we again face the march of the potted plants," he said, looking hard at the two waiters preparing to serve the dinner, "I need to tell you, first, that Heinrich Cutler's medical situation remains pretty much as it has been all along. His condition is stable but the coma continues. However, there is some good news. Through the coordinated intervention of our American friends, the mayor's office, and the American ambassador in the capitol, Heinrich was flown today, along with his parents and his beloved Liz, to the Ramstein air base in Germany. From there, just as with many victims of the Iraq war, he will be transferred to the brain trauma unit which has been doing absolutely pioneer work in restoring the health of brain-injured victims. If Heinrich has a chance for reasonable survival, that is where it will happen. I know he has your prayers, and I truly believe now he is in the best of hands. My American colleague at the table, here, tells me that in the 45 years he has been involved in gang studies, not a single researcher has lost his life on the job. To the extent that you can, please be happy for Heinrich, and please now join us in a festive evening. Thank you."

This was followed by much mumbling and commentary around the room as portions of prosciutto and melon were distributed. Then, with appetizers finished, one of the waiters appeared with a small flower in his hand, and proceeded to count the flowers in the rector's centerpiece bouquet – "…17, 18, 19, 20…" yes, the correct number, so he moved on to the next table. Keller remarked that the guy was so rigid – exactly 20 flowers per table – that he must be Schwabian (southern German, known for rigid fastidiousness). While this was going on, the table was creating its own entertainment. With three glasses of different sizes, bottled water, red wine, and white wine, the group faced the task of getting the proper liquid into the proper glass. The deputy mayor, who presented himself as having some knowledge of such things, declared for putting the red wine in the largest glass. When it subsequently became clear that this decision was incorrect, his wife led the group through a transfer-of-liquids sequence, pouring the red wine from the wrong glass into the right glass, then the water from its wrong glass into the right glass, finally freeing the proper glass for the white wine.

After this exploration of manners, the waiter returned to the table, evidently having placed the lost flower, in order to remove the plates from the starter course. He started removing the American's, but then with a slight look of contempt on his face, he took the American's fork (then lying right side up) and turned it over on the plate. All understood this as a second correction of manners, after the gaffe with the wine glasses. Apparently this was how to place one's utensil to indicate being finished. So several others compliantly turned their forks over, to comply with local custom, and the plates were removed. Somewhat later, the same waiter reappeared to water each table's centerpiece with Evian! Obviously they had a weird character here, but what the heck, the food was good and the wine was flowing (into the correct glasses now).

Next, the waiter returned holding a shoe and indicated that someone had left it somewhere. A woman at the next table presented her foot, but like Cinderella's stepsisters, the shoe did not fit. In this case, it was too big, and the waiter pulled out a pair of scissors, offering to make the shoe fit. By now, it was not clear whether a hiring error had been made by the banquet coordinator, or what. But there was a gradual dawning that they might just be watching a performance.

The next act was the reemergence of the waiter, now missing a shoe on one of his own feet. It was now dessert time, and the two came out of the kitchen trying to manage a very long, metal step ladder that kept getting caught in the door. They placed it up against the tallest of the plants, a thirty-foot rubber tree. But rather than spreading the legs of the ladder, one waiter got under the ladder, bracing it while the other climbed to the top to dust off the leaves of the plant. Trust me – 50 people were at this point out of their skulls, pounding tables and applauding every stupid move.

Of course, when they were through, they attempted to take the ladder back out through the kitchen door, and couldn't find a way to do it. Finally, they just left it against the wall. Last act: the main character came out holding a tray with 2 small bowls of toothpicks. Starting at Keller's table, he explained that one batch is without meat, and the other without cheese. The deputy mayor, attempting to one-up the guy, declared for one with tenderizer; whereupon the waiter reached into his pocket and produced a Q-tip, which he presented to his victim.

It turns out that when Martin Keller suggested the gala dinner, including the usual banquet musicians, Magda mentioned this pair of mimes from Ghent, Belgium and so Keller hired them, without ever having seen them perform. Even he was fooled at first. They also have a routine for outdoor parties, at which they appear as gardeners. Planning a banquet, anyone?

With the lighter touch having now prevailed, people wandered about with some dessert wine in hand as the real waiters began to clear tables. Keller called for attention one last time to announce that he or his American friend would offer a presentation on gang policies and practices to the mayor's panel the following week. All interested parties were invited to attend and participate in a discussion. And with that he thanked everyone again and bade them a good evening. He hadn't noticed that while he was standing, one of the mimes had removed his chair and replaced it with an identical one. Keller wondered why a few people were snickering.

At the door, as everyone filed out, the mimes greeted them with open hats, taking donations. With each contribution they remained silent but bowed deeply. As they in turn gathered their few props, they looked over the banquet hall, now empty but for the real waiters cleaning up. One looked at the other, and at the accumulated donations, and said in heavily accented Flemish, "Well, another day, another dollar. Life goes on." They didn't notice Patrick van der Waal in the darkened corner behind them, note pad in hand, recording their comment as the final quote in his penultimate story on the Eurogang Project.

Selected References

Block, Carolyn Rebecca, and Richard Block. 1993. Street gang crime in Chicago. *Research in Brief.* National Institute of Justice.

Decker, Scott H. and Frank M. Weerman(eds.). 2005. *European Street Gangs and Troublesome Youth Groups.* Lanham, MD: AltaMira Press.

Esbenson, Finn-Aage, David Huizinga, and Anne W. Weiher. 1993. *Journal of Contemporary Criminal Justice.* 9:94-116.

Fleisher, Mark S. 1998. *Dead End Kids: Gang Girls and the Boys They Know.* Madison: University of Wisconsin Press.

Junger-Tas, Josine, Gert-Jan Terlouw, and Malcolm W. Klein (eds.). 1994. *Delinquent Behavior Among Young People in the Western World.* Amsterdam: Kugler Publications.

Klein, Malcolm W. 1995. *The American Street Gang: Its Nature, Prevalence, and Control.* Oxford: Oxford University Press.

Klein, Malcolm W. 2004. *Gang Cop: The Words and Ways of Officer Paco Domingo.* Walnut Creek: AltaMira Press.

Klein, Malcolm W. 2007. *Chasing After Street Gangs: A Forty-Year Journey.* Upper Saddle River, N.J.: Pearson Prentice-Hall.

Klein, Malcolm W., Hans-Jeurgen Kerner, Cheryl L. Maxson, and Elmar G.M. Weitekamp(eds.). 2001. *The Eurogang Paradox: Street Gangs and Youth Groups in the U.S. and Europe.* Dordrecht: Kluwer Academic Publishers.

Klein, Malcolm W. and Cheryl Maxson. 2006. *Street Gang Patterns and Policies.* Oxford: Oxford University Press.

Klein, Malcolm W., Frank M. Weerman, and Terence P. Thornberry. 2006. Street gang violence in Europe. *European Journal of Criminology.* 3(4): 413-437.

Maxson, Cheryl L. 2001. A proposal for multi-site study of European gangs and youth groups. In Klein et al(eds.), *Supra.*

Patrick, James. 1973. *A Glascow Gang Observed.* London: Eyre Methuen.

Tertilt, Hermann. 2001. Patterns of ethnic violence in a Frankfurt street gang. In Klein et al, *Supra.*

van Gemert, Frank F., Dana Peterson, and Inger-Lise Lien(eds.). 2008. *Youth Gangs, Migration, and Ethnicity.* Devon: Willan Publishing.

Vercaigne, Conny. 2001. The group aspect of crime and youth gangs in Brussels: What do we know and especially what we don't know. In Klein et al, *Supra.*

Yablonsky, Lewis. 1963. *The Violent Gang.* New York: Macmillan.